SLAYER

Dragon Tamer Book 1

Armitage & Culican

Edited by: Cassidy Taylor

ISBN-13: 978-1546705529

ISBN-10: 154670552x

www.dragonrealmpress.com

To our daughters…

May you grow to be brave and strong

SLAYER

CONTENTS

CHAPTER ONE

I held the sword up in the air as the sun glinted off of it, blinding me for the briefest of seconds. That was something I'd have to watch out for in the future. It was also heavier than I expected it to be after unofficially training for so long with the old, battered swords. Normal swords. Boring swords. But this was no ordinary weapon. Apart from being the traditional sword of my family and my eighteenth birthday present to boot, I knew it to be hollowed out down the thickest part of the main shaft.

"You aren't going to kill a dragon holding it up in the air like that, Julianna," Jasper said with a smirk. "Do you expect them to just fly down from the sky and impale themselves on it?"

I lowered my sword and stuck my tongue out at my brother. At nineteen, he was exactly one year and one day older than me, a fact he liked to lord over me at all given opportunities. He was also taller, more popular, and downright annoying.

"Jasper, leave your sister alone. This time last year I seem to remember you nearly slicing off your big toe. We all have to start somewhere." My father's voice boomed toward us.

Jasper's smirk transformed into a scowl and I snickered. I knew why he had a bee in his bonnet but it was hardly my fault. He had also received a sword for his eighteenth birthday which was practically identical to mine. Both had our family crest and a dragon forged onto the handle, the eyes inlaid with our birthstones. If he'd been born a day later or I'd been born a day earlier, they would be exactly the same. As it was, his had eyes of jet, a common element found naturally in the Triad Mountains, while my dragon's eyes glittered with fire diamonds, an infinitely rare and therefore more expensive jewel. Both swords cost more than the average family in Dronios paid in a month's rent, but thanks to the two fire diamonds, mine could also feed and clothe them for the same month if I ever had any inclination to sell it, which, of course, I never would.

"Now!" My father clapped me on the shoulder nearly causing me to drop the sword. "Your brother is going to show you some moves so you can get used to the weight and feel of it and when I think you're ready, the two of you will spar. I don't expect you to win but I do expect you to pay attention to what Jasper tells you and to at least block him. Do you understand?"

"Yes, Papa!" I turned to him and, lifting myself up on my tiptoes, kissed him on the cheek.

"Come here, baby sister. I'll show you how a real warrior holds a sword." Jasper's tight voice met my ears.

The dust swirled around my feet as I crossed the training ground to him. I idly wondered if my father would declare me the winner if I stuck the sword right in his only son's gut. Okay, probably not, but it was a nice thought.

"You're holding your sword like a girl," he said, taking it out of my hands.

"If I hold my sword like Morganna, then I'll be quite happy," I replied. The legendary swordswoman brought men to their knees both figuratively and literally. Holding my sword like a girl indeed!

He took hold of my hand and placed the sword back into it, this time in a slightly different position. Damn it, it did feel better.

"Now, when I give you the say so, lift your sword and copy the pose I show you."

I waited until he picked up his own sword and got himself into a position I knew to be a blocking stance. One foot was slightly behind the other to steady him, should he need it. He angled his left arm behind him while his right held his sword out in front of him so that it crossed his chest. I followed his lead and put myself in position, but as I did, it didn't feel quite right. I wasn't steady enough. My feet weren't far enough apart and if I was in a real sword fight, I'd left too many parts of myself exposed. I widened my stance slightly.

"Pay attention Jules," Jasper snapped. "This is important."

I looked over my shoulder to see that my father was still exactly where I left him, watching us with his hand held up to block the glare of the sun. It was important for me to do exactly what Jasper said. I didn't want to let my father down. Closing the distance between my feet, I tried to position myself exactly how my brother stood.

"That's better. You're learning already!"

He took me through more blocking stances before he moved on to other forms of defense. After an hour and a half of protecting myself—mainly from barbed comments from my brother, but occasionally from pretend jabs of his sword—I began to tire.

"I'm done with defense. You're teaching me to protect myself against another swordsman, but we'll be chasing dragons. I need to learn how to attack." I was being childish but he was treating me like a child and I was annoyed.

"The concept is the same. You'll still have to defend yourself against dragons."

I couldn't see how any of the moves he'd just taught me would help me if a dragon decided to flame me.

"Go get yourself a drink of water if you're fading," he said, his mouth twisting back into its spiteful smirk. "We'll start on attacking moves in five minutes." His eyebrows narrowed and he turned away, effectively dismissing me.

I didn't want to admit it to him, but I did need a break. The sword was much heavier than the ones I was used to practicing with. I'd actually started my training a year ago on the same day Jasper did, watching him and my father from my bedroom window, wishing I was old enough to join them. The next day, as I was grabbing seedlings from the shed, I found an old practice sword and took it for myself. The feel of the sword as my hand grabbed the hilt that first time was seared into my brain, the strength and power that it represented burned into my being. Every day, I watched Jasper's training sessions and then practiced the same moves in my bedroom. Today I'd finally be sparring with a real person and not just the shadows.

I grabbed the jug that had been left on an old wooden table and poured myself a goblet of water and one each for Jasper and Papa. The water was warm after being out in the burning sun, but it refreshed me all the same.

"You're doing well, little one." My father took his goblet and drank before pulling a face. "This would be better if it was ice cold ale."

"Yes, but then you'd be too drunk to watch me kick Jasper's a— butt, and please don't call me little one. I'm eighteen today, a woman now!"

Papa just laughed at me but Jasper had heard what I said and turned from where he'd been practicing his footwork. He took the third goblet and drained it easily. "I think you'll be lucky to block me at all, let alone kick anything," he said. "I'll have yours on the ground before you know what's hit you."

"Now, now, you two," Papa started before draining his drink. "Save your squabble for the fight."

I put my goblet down and stalked back to the center of the dusty training ground to wait for

Jasper. I did love him. He was my only brother after all, but he was a complete and utter pain in the neck.

I stalked around the training circle kicking up more dirt as I took in my surroundings. Our home sat on the outskirts of Dronios, the small village my family had belonged to since the beginning of time. The Triad Mountains hovered in the background with the promise of power only a dragon could bring me. The only known place dragons lived.

Two hours later and he'd shown me every move he knew, both attack and defense, and watched as I'd practiced each one ten times. The sun was considerably lower in the sky when Papa came over to us. I was glad that the heat of the day had gone with the lowering sun, but now that it was directly behind Jasper, I had a hard time seeing him, and he, of course, refused to move.

"I think you've worked hard enough today," Papa said as he wrapped an arm around my sweaty shoulders. "I'm going to let you spar, but Julianna, you should use the moves you've learned today to block. If you think you can get an attack in, by all means, go for it but I don't expect you to get a hit in."

"Yeah, like that's going to happen," said Jasper as he pulled on his training armor. "I don't know why I'm even putting this on." He smirked at me as I lifted up the armor set aside for me.

"Don't wear it. I just hope you got enough birthday money yesterday for your healer's bill," I retorted.

"Children!" My father rolled his eyes at us and a pit of unease grew in my stomach. I wanted him to be proud of me, not think I was a pathetic little girl.

"Sorry, Papa." I lowered my head.

Jasper picked up his sword and walked to the circle drawn in chalk on the ground.

"Papa?"

"Yes, my girl?"

"How can this be a fair fight?" I picked up my sword, now much more comfortable with its weight.

"This is your first day. I expect it will take you months, if not years, to be as good as your brother.

He is becoming quite well known for his swordsmanship. He will not hurt you."

"That's not exactly what I meant." It irked me that my father was expecting so little of me. "Jasper's sword has been imbued with the soul of his first dragon kill. Mine is still empty."

"What do you suggest? I can ask your brother to swap swords if you like but even though his sword gives him strength from the dragon, which will pass to you if you have it, I'm still certain he'll beat you."

"I don't want his sword. That won't be fair either. I want to use yours." It was unbelievably cheeky of me to ask. I wouldn't normally have dared, but I was beginning to get angry with both my father and Jasper for treating me like I was a hopeless case.

He looked down to where the sword was sheathed by his side. It had been forged in the Triad Mountains over thirty years ago by the goblins that mined there. The legendary blade was made from the rarest metal of all and had won the soul of over three hundred dragons. I'd never once seen it leave my father's side. He stared at me as he rolled the idea over in his head.

My hopes began to rise. Would he really let me borrow it?

"No, Julianna. I cannot let you use my sword."

That was that then. I was going into a fight at a disadvantage before I even started. I could have cried.

"But," my father continued, "I do understand your point of view. You are right. You must do this fairly. Jasper!" he called out to my brother who ran back over to us.

"Don't tell me she's chickened out." He grinned.

"Hand me your sword. You'll both use old training swords of mine. They aren't quite as heavy as these swords, but they are identical to each other which will make the fight fair."

Jasper's face fell and now I was the one grinning.

"I'll get them, Papa. Where do you keep them?" I asked innocently. I could hardly tell either of them that I'd had one of them in my possession for a year.

"They're in a shed behind the house."

I ran around the house to the back where I retrieved one of the swords. Thankfully we had a back door, so neither of them would see me running up to my bedroom to retrieve the other from under my bed where it had laid hidden for the past twelve months. I brought both swords back outside and handed them to my father.

He took something small out of his pocket and dabbed it on the tip of one of the swords.

"What's that, Papa?" I queried.

"This ink will show up as a blue mark every time Jasper hits your armor. The less blue you have on you at the end of the duel, the more successful you've been at defending yourself."

"Just make sure you put it on my sword too," I replied. I might not have been fighting to attack but my father had told me I could try.

Jasper still had a sour expression on his face when he took up the starting position. I faced him and bowed. The niceties should always be followed in any duel, even one where everyone thinks you are going to lose. Jasper bowed too.

"On my whistle," I heard my father say, but I didn't break eye contact with Jasper.

"One, two, three." The shrill call of the whistle blared as my father backed away. Immediately, Jasper lunged at me. I blocked him but only just in time. He wasn't playing. He was really trying to hurt me! Papa obviously thought the same because he blew the whistle a second time to signal the end of the duel. The quickest duel ever, after which Jasper would get a telling off for going too hard on me and I'd get a pat on the back for blocking him.

No, this wasn't how this was going to go down. I ignored the whistle and thrust my sword forward. It was designed to put him off guard and it worked. He wasn't ready for me. He looked over at Papa with a raised eyebrow. I flicked my eyes over to see my father's expression. He shrugged his shoulders as if to say, "Carry on." Fine! Carry on I would!

Jasper pulled his features back into a sneer and lunged again. This time I was ready for him. I didn't need to block; I was too quick for that. By the time his sword should have hit the armor covering my stomach, I was five inches to the right. I hopped

19

around to his back and planted my first blue dot right in the middle of his shoulder blades. He whipped his sword around but I saw it coming and ducked, rolling around to his front. Before he had the chance to defend himself, I plunged the sword forward again, this time staining a spot on his chest. Papa's laugh echoed around me, fueling my movements. He was enjoying this, as was I.

"Beginner's luck, Jules," spat Jasper as he lunged forward trying a fancy move he'd not bothered to show me.

So, that's how you want to play it, huh? I blocked his sword, which he anticipated, and pulled back only to lunge again straight away. I had some fancy footwork of my own and after blocking him a second time, I was able to attack again. I drew dot after dot all over his armor and it was only when my father blew the whistle again that I was able to truly see just how much damage I'd done to Jasper.

He was covered in hundreds of tiny, blue kisses. When I looked down, my armor was still the plain gray it had always been.

"Julianna," Papa said, striding over to us. "That was amazing! How did you do that?"

"She got lucky, that's all." Jasper scowled and threw his armor onto the ground along with the old sword.

"Lucky? You have more blue on you than the Parvanian Ocean." I couldn't help but gloat.

Jasper's scowl got meaner and he stormed off into the house, leaving Papa and me to clean up.

"Should I take his sword back to him?" I asked as I grabbed his jet sword off the ground.

"No, give him some space. You embarrassed him out there. I'm so proud of you. I just didn't think...I mean I didn't expect..."

"It's fine Papa. I surprised myself too if I'm honest."

"I feel bad for underestimating you. It's not something you will have to worry about again. I'm taking you out tomorrow."

"Out?" I asked, picking up the armor that Jasper had thrown down.

21

"Into the mountains. You're going to fill up that sword of yours. It needs the soul of a dragon and you're going to be the one to put it there."

I looked at my father incredulously. It had taken Jasper nine months from getting his sword to having his first kill.

"I'm not ready, Papa!"

"Twenty minutes ago, I'd have agreed with that statement. You've shown me how wrong I can be and I'm sorry."

"You're sure?"

He put his arm around my shoulder and handed me my fire diamond sword. The final rays of the sun glinted for the last time that day.

"My love, I've never been surer of anything in my life."

CHAPTER TWO

awn sent rays of sunshine filtering through the ragged curtains in my bedroom. I jumped out of bed with an air of trepidation. Fear mingled with excitement as I pondered the day ahead. Today was my first hunt, the most important day for any dragon slayer. It was the most important job anyone in our village could have. The job all younglings yearned for. The one I was destined to have since the day of my birth, thanks to my slayer parents.

I checked my reflection in the mirror. Long wavy hair cascading around my shoulders was completely inappropriate for any slayer. I was

23

going on a hunt, not to a party. I tied it on top of my head in a messy bun and turned my attention to the clothes that I'd left out the night before. They were actually pretty basic—khaki colored leggings with a similar colored tunic and a thick, brown leather belt that my mother had bought me for my birthday. The shield of our family was engraved on the buckle, complete with the requisite silver dragon. It had the same fire diamond eyes as my sword so I knew to keep it away from Jasper.

The floor shook as Jasper stomped around his room next door, no doubt still being the sore loser he was yesterday. Thunderous footsteps on the stairs followed by a slamming door told me he had left the house. I peeked out and sure enough, Jasper was stalking across the training ground towards the road that would take him to the village less than a quarter mile up the road. He was already covered in armor with his sword sheathed neatly at his hip, and I'd not even had breakfast yet. As if on cue, there was a knock at my door and my mother's small voice came through.

"Julianna. Honey, I've brought you some breakfast. I thought you might need it today."

I opened the door and kissed my mother on the cheek before taking the plate of bacon and eggs from her and setting it on my vanity desk.

At just under four feet, she was the smallest person in the village and the most unlikely dragon slayer my family had produced. I couldn't imagine her out of her flowery dresses and the white apron she always wore.

"I'm not sure I can eat anything, Mom, I'm too nervous!"

"I was watching you out there yesterday. You put your brother to shame, not that I'd ever tell him that. I have faith you'll be an excellent dragon slayer just like the generations of Slayers before you."

"How did you do it, Mom?" With her small size and gentle personality, I doubted she'd be able to pick up my sword, let alone wield it at a dragon.

"Oh, I was hopeless," she said with a grin. "The sword was almost as big as I was and I was a complete bag of nerves. I honestly thought I was going to cause an avalanche with all the quivering I was doing walking up that mountain with your grandfather. And then we saw it. It was the biggest, ugliest mountain dragon you ever saw in your life and it was angry. Your grandfather charged at it, sword blazing, but tripped over a stone and knocked himself out." She giggled as she replayed the memory.

"So, it was just you and the dragon?" I'd never heard this story before. My father told us stories all the time about his escapades but my mother was usually quiet on the subject.

She nodded her head. "I almost turned and ran down the mountain but I couldn't leave my father."

My eyes widened at the thought. "So, what did you do?"

"I pulled out a slingshot I'd borrowed from your uncle. He was eight years old at the time and had given it to me for good luck. I found a stone and shot it right at the dragon's eye." She chuckled quietly. "I got a clear shot and half-blinded the thing. He must have been disorientated because he began to rampage, spewing flames everywhere. I managed to pull my father into a crevice and the stupid dragon ended up setting himself on fire.

"When the flames died down a bit and it looked like my father was stirring, I picked up my sword and plunged it into the dragon. My father opened his eyes and thought I'd fought with the dragon. I wasn't about to dispel the notion. I told him that night that I couldn't bring myself to do it again. He was just so proud of his dragon-slaying daughter that he let me be." She took my hand and stroked it. "I've never told another soul that story so I'm hoping you'll see fit to keep it to yourself. Your grandfather will never forgive me if he knew the truth."

I couldn't help it. I laughed loudly then flung my arms around my mother.

"Just so you know there is more than one way to skin a cat, or kill a dragon in this case. Now eat up, they'll be waiting for you in the village."

I wolfed down the breakfast and my nerves dissipated. If my mother could do it, then I surely could. So what if she cheated a little? The end result was the same. Maybe I'd take some of her luck onto the mountain with me today.

The armor was much trickier than the clothes had been. Every piece weighed me down, heavy with flame repellent magic. There were buckles to fasten and ties to knot and as each piece was put on, my ability to actually move became more and more impaired. I had no idea how I was going to manage to walk down the stairs, let alone climb a mountain. When my father came to see if I was ready and then kindly told me I'd put it all on backward, I was relieved to find that it was much easier to wear correctly. He handed me the weapons that would fasten to my belt—an 8-inch dagger and a water-logged grenade. Finally, he passed me my sword so I could fit it into its sheath. In a few hours' time, after it was weighed down with the soul of a dragon, it would be the heaviest piece of equipment I possessed.

My mother kissed my cheek and I felt her slip something into my pocket. I had a pretty good idea what. She winked and I left the house, ready for my adventure to begin. The walk to the village was a slow one. My father showed endless patience as I kept stopping to adjust something. Getting used to this armor was going to be tricky.

Dust on the road swirled around my feet, dry from months of sunshine. It would have been so much easier if I'd been born in Spring or Autumn when the air was cooler, but no, I was born at the peak of the year, when the sun was at its hottest. I reminded myself that it was a day much like today, not too long ago, when Jasper had done his first kill and I'd already proved I could do better than him. I only hoped I didn't let my father down. I understood my mother's reluctance to tell her story. I needed to prove myself at all costs.

Music met my ears as signs of a celebration began at the very outer reaches of the village. Red and gold bunting was strung from post to post. Excitement flooded through me at the thought of what lay ahead. I knew that when I got further into the town center, there would be banners hung from windows and lamp posts with my name on them. All the villagers would come out to greet me, to wish me well for my big day. It was a small village so it wasn't often someone turned eighteen. Before Jasper, it had been three years since they had been able to put on a party like this. And what parties they were.

The newer slayers who had already acquired their dragon soul would go up into the mountains with the birthday boy or girl, but they were only there for back up. It was up to the person whose birthday it was to make the first kill. Of course, the village never knew when the festivities would begin since it depended on when during their eighteenth year they were ready for their first kill. Those left behind would spend the day baking and preparing for the celebration that was to come. A huge space on the village green was always left for the body of the dragon, and around the edges would be tables full of delicious food. Musicians would perform on the small stage and everyone would dance late into the night.

A sudden thought hit me and memories of celebrations drifted away.

"What happens if we don't find a dragon?" I actually wanted to ask what would happen if I didn't kill one but I didn't want to appear weak.

"You can always find a dragon, as long as you know where to look," he replied heartily.

"But what if—"

"Julianna, I've lived in this village for forty-eight years. I've been to so many of these celebrations, I've lost count I'd be lying if I said there haven't been one or two injuries along the way, but I've never—not once—seen a new slayer come back down from those mountains without a dragon. Hell, your mother managed it with her kid brother's slingshot!"

"She told me that this morning. She said you didn't know."

"Honey, everyone knows. I personally think it's the best dragon killing story I've ever heard, God bless her."

I smiled. There had never been a single new hunt without a dragon. It made me feel better until a niggling thought bored its way into my brain. What if I was the first?

"Don't you worry about a thing," Papa said as he placed his hand on my shoulder. "After today, you will know everything there is to know about being a slayer. Today, you will learn our secrets." He winked and strolled to the center of the square.

It seemed everyone had come out to greet me. I could barely move for the shouts of "Good luck!" and claps on the back. Smiles were aplenty as I shook hands and nodded graciously to the excited crowd. I breathed deeply and tried to hold back my nerves as words of congratulations were thrown at me. As the crowd thinned, I made out Jasper sitting on an old marker stone sharpening his already sharp sword. He still had the same grouchy look on his face that he'd had when I beat him yesterday.

I scanned the other villagers, looking for the slayers who would be accompanying me up the mountain. There were so many people milling around it was difficult to see them all, but the tell-tale armor that slayers wore was visible here and there between all the other people.

"It's time, slayers!" someone shouted, and as if by magic, the crowd parted and the slayers congregated on the small patch of scorched grass that surrounded Jasper's stone.

I walked forward to join them, knowing all eyes would be on me. There was no need for introductions. I'd grown up with them, but it didn't stop each and every one of them coming up to me and shaking my hand. Well, all except for Jasper who just looked at me moodily.

I gazed up at the Triad Mountains. They looked spectacular in the bright morning sunshine. The middle of the three had snow on its peak, even in the summer sun. I'd never been allowed to climb higher than the village border before, marked by a fence that had been dug into the hard earth before I was born. I'd spent so much time looking up to these mountains, dreaming of the day I'd finally be able to conquer them, and now that day was here at last. I gulped at the thought of what lie ahead but a couple of deep breaths calmed my nerves. I was ready.

I put my best foot forward and took the lead to the sounds of cheering behind me. The wonderful energy provided by the remaining villagers buoyed me.

The fence beckoned to me in the distance and so I marched purposely forward toward my destiny.

"You might have beaten me, little sister," Jasper hissed into my ear. "But fighting me doesn't compare to fighting a dragon. You're not ready; you will fail."

I ignored him. He might be known as the strongest newbie slayer in the village, but as I looked up to the sun-bathed mountains, I knew that I'd prove him wrong yet.

Chapter Three

The hike up the mountain was more taxing than I thought it would be. I was fit but I hadn't been given time to get used to the weight of all the armor. To take my mind off the struggle, I admired the view around me. At the other side of the village border was a thick band of giant evergreen fir trees that appeared to give the mountain a skirt. It was cooler under the shade of them which I was thankful for, but it wouldn't last. I unhooked a canteen of water from my belt and took a deep swig.

"Not so fast, Julianna!" said Marcus, one of the boys from the village. "We have a long way to go yet and dehydration will kill you faster than an angry dragon if you aren't careful."

I slipped the lid back on and put the canteen away. I knew to listen to the more experienced members of the group. At twenty-three, Marcus was one of the younger ones but he'd been on enough of these expeditions to know what he was talking about. Brown pine needles carpeted the ground beneath us, making it soft and springy. Sounds of wildlife filled the air, birds in the trees and hidden animals scurrying in the undergrowth.

I turned to Marcus. "Why is the village border below the tree line? It's beautiful in here. Surely dragons don't come into the woods."

"They don't, but once we get out of the trees the terrain changes dramatically and that's when you know you need to keep your wits about you. It's rare that they come so low down the mountain but it's not unheard of. You'll see one or two scorched trees at the upper border. That's the work of dragons!"

Light filtered through the dense copse of trees much more freely now as we neared the upper edge of the woods. In a couple of minutes, I might be coming face to face with a dragon for the first time.

Fear whipped through me and adrenaline pumped through my body. Scorched trees? I knew how to wield a sword but what good did that do against flames?

"What if the dragon breathes fire in my direction?" I asked him, feeling woefully under-educated.

"You duck!" he replied. "Quickly!"

Great! I could barely stand up straight in the armor, I wasn't sure I'd be able to duck, and I was positive that even if I managed it, I wouldn't be able to do it quickly.

I didn't have time to panic as the trees gave way to a rocky gray terrain. Occasional weeds and the odd hardy flower grew between the cracks in the stones but that was the only sign of life. I tried to ignore the black marks on some of the rocks. Burn marks.

The air turned from the sweet-smelling fragrance of pine to a faint acrid smell.

"What's that smell?" I asked, turning my nose up.

"You'd better get used to it. It's the smell of sulfur. It gets stronger the higher up you go. It's the smell of dragons." I turned to see Marcus grinning. He was enjoying this a lot more than I was.

If I ignored the smell and immediate barren terrain, it was actually pretty beautiful up here. Once we'd cleared the treeline, I could see far into the distance. Looking back, I picked out our house with smoke coming out of the chimney, no doubt thanks to my mother's baking. The village was tiny from this high but I could still make out the colors of all of the banners and decorations for the party tonight.

I couldn't look behind me for too long, because like Marcus had told me, I needed to keep my wits about me. The last thing I needed was to be flame-grilled when I was too busy admiring the view.

The skies above me were clear except for the odd wispy cloud that scudded across the sky. It was perfect slaying weather. Occasionally, from the village, I had seen dragons flying around the peaks but they were often so far away, they looked like birds, but there were none flying about today. I'd only ever seen dragons from such a distance that they were no more than dots in the sky, or the dead ones brought back to the village. I'd grown up surrounded by lore of dragons and I knew everything about them except anything practical.

Three hours later and the terrain had become even more difficult to climb. Rocky outcrops and caves were everywhere so, although Marcus had told me to keep my wits about me, I didn't really know where to look. It seemed like a dragon could be hiding waiting to pounce from anywhere, and there was evidence of them dotted all around us in the form of the discarded bones and carcasses of small mammals. The heat and the smell of sulfur intensified, and it was all I could do not to pass out. The trek was so much more grueling than I had expected and I'd already guzzled my way through half my water rations.

My father who had been walking ahead stopped suddenly and raised his arm as a signal for us to follow suit.

"There is a well-known dragon roost just round those rocks there," whispered Marcus. "It's where I got my first kill. Good luck!"

For the first time, the fear that had been plaguing me throughout the entire trek turned into full-on terror. My time was nearly here. Just another fifty or so more steps and I'd be face to face with my first dragon. My father beckoned me forward. I'd be expected to go in there first.

I put one foot in front of the other and began to walk forward.

"Good luck, little sister," hissed my brother as I passed him. "Don't let the dragon burn you on the butt!" He laughed lightly but I held my head up and ignored him. I might be quivering on the inside but I wasn't going to give him the satisfaction of knowing that.

"Julianna," my father said, clapping me on the shoulder with his huge hands and nearly shaking some of my armor off in the process. "Whatever happens up there, I just want you to know I'm proud of you. I'll be behind you the whole time and you've got the others as back up. If we see you struggling, we'll step in but I want you to do everything to get that dragon without our help. Only that way will you capture his soul. You don't want to fight him almost to the death and then have someone else come in to finish the job. You have to be the one. Do you understand me?"

"Yes, father."

"The carcasses here are fresh and the scorch marks on the rocks are old. That means there hasn't been any other slayer up here for a while. They only breathe fire if they feel threatened. Now go on in there and do your best!"

I managed a half-hearted smile and set off up the rocks alone. Harsh breathing came from behind me although there was no sound of footsteps. Either they were being incredibly quiet or they were giving me a head start. I didn't turn to see which.

Pulling myself up the last ten feet or so, I peeked my head around the corner, wondering what exactly I'd come face to face with. It could be anything from a small immature Triad dragon to a fully grown Royal Scarlet Flame, the biggest and deadliest breed of dragon in our kingdom.

At first, I thought the crevasse was empty. An old roost built from reeds and stones was perched under a rocky outcrop which had been blackened by years of dragonfire, but there was none in sight. I breathed a sigh of relief until I realized it meant more climbing until we found one. I was just about to turn and let the hunting party know when I spotted something in the middle of the roost. I moved forward cautiously to get a closer look. At first, I thought it might be a huge pearl from the giant oysters that lived off the coast of our land, but when I peered over the edge of the roost I saw it for what it was. A dragon's egg. Its opalescent shell glimmered in the noonday sun.

I was confused for a second. Why would there be a dragon's egg without a mother dragon? But then a huge screech from above me told me there wasn't. I looked up to see the whole sky above me had turned scarlet.

CHAPTER FOUR

I stood rooted to the spot. Now was my time to shine but I had absolutely no clue what to do. My training went right out the window. The dark red dragon circled above, dropping lower and lower in the sky but it was nowhere near close enough to impale with my sword. How did the others do this? More importantly, why didn't I know how to do this? I'd been waiting my whole life for this and now I couldn't even move, let alone slay a dragon. I felt like a kid on the first day of school.

My mother's story came back to me and I remembered the thing she'd slipped into my pocket. I already knew what it was but I still felt relief when I pulled out the slingshot. I scoured the ground quickly for a loose stone of the correct size, grabbing the first one I found and fitting it into the pouch.

The dragon had seen me, I was sure of it, but it hadn't attacked yet. I pulled back hard on the leather string of the slingshot, ready to fire, when a hand grabbed hold of my belt from behind and pulled me backward so fast I ended up stumbling and then falling, sending both me and the person behind me flying back down the rocks.

"What are you doing?" I hissed angrily, turning to find Jasper rubbing his head after banging it in the fall.

"Are you a complete moron?" he asked, pulling himself up and dusting himself off.

I gave him a look of disgust before doing the same myself. "What are you talking about?"

"What do you think is going to happen if you use that children's toy?" he spat. "Do you seriously think a small stone will fall a dragon? Because if you do, you are out of your mind."

Anger coursed through me. "Okay, hotshot. What else was I supposed to do? Wait for it to land and bring out a white flag? If you hadn't noticed, it was up in the air!"

It was then I noted that we were alone. "Where is everyone else?"

"They've gone around the other way." He pointed to a rough trail at the side of the rocky outcrop. "You can climb up onto the higher rocks up there which will put us about even with the dragon. Father told me to come get you. I guess he knew you'd make a mess of it."

That really stung. I needed to make my father proud.

"Right then," I said, setting off briskly up the path he'd pointed out. "Are you coming or not?"

The dragon was now completely out of sight but I could hear it. With each step I took, the noise of the flapping wings grew louder. The path was steep and shaded by the cliff to my right that turned into the cleft that the dragon was flying over. I could see Jasper's point. If I kept climbing up, I would be much closer to where the dragon was, making it a much easier target. I pulled myself up the last bit and found myself on the very top of the rocky outcrop that formed the cliff. The others all stood there, swords raised ready to fight. To my surprise, the dragon was still circling around, seemingly oblivious to the men poised to kill it.

My father saw me and beckoned me over. "We waited for you. You have to be the one to kill it. I must warn you, a Royal Scarlet Flame is not the easiest kill. Usually, they attack without warning and shoot fire without being provoked. This one is acting very strangely. You might be in luck, it could be sick. I've never known one not to attack before."

"Maybe it hasn't seen us yet?" I guessed.

"It's seen us all right. It's even flown past a couple of times close enough for us to kill it but you have to be the one to do that. If it's sick, you're going to have an easy job. Just go to the edge of the cliff and wait for it to circle back around. When it gets near, you'll need to stab it. Go for the brain or the heart. If you get it anywhere else, you've effectively given yourself a death sentence."

I'd felt better for a minute but it's funny how phrases such as "death sentence" can instill fear into someone.

The others moved back when I approached, giving me room to run if I needed to. Walking slowly towards the edge of the cliff, I kept my eyes on the dragon, making sure I had room to move if he breathed fire. To my immediate front and about five meters to my right were sheer cliffs. I peeked behind me to see that the slayers had formed a line, keeping their distance while ready to spring into action. I inched closer to the edge, my gaze returning to the dragon. He was still lazily flying around, sometimes ducking into the crevasse below. I wondered if its behavior had something to do with the egg. Perhaps it didn't want to fight us on the cliff for fear that someone else would harm its precious egg? Were dragons really that clever?

My feet came to the very edge of the cliff. One misstep and it wouldn't be the dragon I had to worry about. I hazarded a peek downward and immediately felt dizzy. The valley below was nothing more than a green blur. I'd been gearing up my whole life to be a slayer, but no one had thought to give me lessons on heights. I could see the egg about thirty meters below me. A fall from this height would undoubtedly kill me. Instinctively I took a step backward and a few deep breaths to clear my head. The dragon flew right past me. A rush of air pulled some of my fiery hair from its bun, obscuring my view for a couple of seconds. Pushing my hair back out of my face, my eyes followed as it once again circled around.

"For goodness' sake, kill it!" Jasper shouted from behind me. "Even a toddler could have gotten it that time."

He was right. I'd missed my chance. I'd not even unsheathed my sword, but the dragon circled around again. There would be another chance and this time I'd not fail to take it. My heart rate increased as I put one foot in front of the other to steady myself and drew my sword. This was it. It was now or never. The dark ruby-colored dragon turned back around, flying towards me in the same trajectory as before. For whatever reason, it was planning another swoop past rather than an attack.

Maybe I was lucky and it really was sick. It certainly wasn't acting as I'd expected it to. As it flew in my direction, I looked into its eyes and poised myself to fight.

I thrust my sword forward but at the very last second, I hesitated, missing the dragon's chest by millimeters. For the briefest of moments, time stood still. It was just me and the dragon. The dragon I was there to kill and yet there was a voice deep within me screaming not to harm her. She was just protecting her egg, just as any other mother would.

"What are you doing?" Jasper screamed behind me. I turned to see a grim expression on my father's face and my brother hopping up and down in ill-hidden anger.

I turned back to the retreating dragon. What had I done? Or should I say why hadn't I done it? Jasper had been right again. Anyone could have killed that dragon, but I'd hesitated. It just didn't feel right killing it when it wasn't able to defend itself. If it was sick, it had no way to fight against me. That should have made me feel happy but it didn't. This should have been easy but it wasn't. My thoughts returned to the egg and I found myself feeling sorry for the dragon.

"Stop it!" I hissed to myself under my breath. "It's a dragon. You're a slayer."

I blew out a harsh breath and focused my mind, mentally psyching myself up to really kill it this time. Sunlight bounced off the dragon's red scales as it began its trip back my way. I pulled myself as tall as I could and readied my sword again. As the dragon came closer I primed myself for the kill. This time I wouldn't hesitate. I pulled back my sword ready to strike when I felt someone running up to me.

"If you can't kill it, I can!" It was Jasper shouting behind me.

Everything happened in a split second that seemed to go on for a thousand years. As the dragon flew past, Jasper's sword glinted in the corner of my eye. I didn't know what inspired me to do it—whether some misguided empathy for the mother dragon or the fact I didn't want him to take my kill, I'll never know—but I ran to the side, blocking him. We crashed into each other and the blow knocked me right over the edge and into the valley below. As I felt myself falling to my death, my father's voice called my name, dying in strength the further I fell.

"Julianna!"

I landed much earlier and on much softer ground than I expected and it took me a couple of seconds to comprehend I was still alive. In my disoriented state, it was a couple more before I realized I'd landed on the dragon's back. It was no accident. It must have seen what happened and flown to catch me. It went against everything I knew about dragons. They were monstrous killing machines. I flipped over so I was the right way up and grabbed hold of the dragon's spines that ran the length of her back. It would be so easy to kill it now but that would send both of us tumbling to our deaths.

We soared into the air and then back towards the men we left behind. Fear etched on their faces as a huge blast of flame erupted from the dragon's mouth, scattering them as we flew past. It took a swoop into the gorge and then out into the open air, leaving my family and the troop behind.

Well, as far as messing up a dragon slaying goes, I think I could definitely claim to be the best. Not only had I failed to kill it, I was now riding on its back to goodness knows where with no way to get down without plummeting to my death. I decided the only thing I could do was hold on for dear life and pray that it landed soon.

The scenery was stunning although I was too scared to really appreciate it as I forced my eyes to stay open and not squeeze closed in fright. Red light bathed the flatlands to the right as we soared over the gray rise of the mountains in front of us. It was heading up to the highest peak of the Triad Mountains. None of my people had ever ventured this far before. There were enough dragons to kill on the lower mountains that we didn't bother coming this high.

We were now flying lower in the sky as if coming into land. The snowy peak of the mountain was still some ways ahead of us but we were miles above where we had left the others behind. The dragon pulled back slightly to slow down as we landed gracefully on a ledge near a cave entrance. At the last possible second, I jumped down and waved my sword around in a very unpracticed manner, all thoughts of my training completely forgotten.

The dragon was about fifteen feet in front of me. I glanced around. The ledge was only about fifty feet long with sheer cliffs dropping away to the right and the same rising above me to the left. If I did nothing, it would kill me. If I killed it, I'd be trapped on the ledge and die anyway.

What a stupid position to find myself in.

I was just weighing my limited options when the dragon made the most sickening sound. Its bones crunched and its skin seemed to fall inwards. Well, Father was right, it really was sick. It looked like it was dying on the spot with no help from me. I wanted to watch to make sure I was ready if it attacked, but it quickly became apparent it was in no position to do so. I closed my eyes, unable to look at it as it let out the most agonizing scream of pain. The grinding of bones turned into a sickening squelching sound that made me feel sick to my stomach and deathly afraid. When it was finally silent, I opened one eye to take a peek.

What I saw before me was not the dead dragon but a man lying face down on the ground.

CHAPTER FIVE

here had he come from? And where was the dragon?

I scoured the skies, both confused and worried. Whatever had just happened had happened so quickly, my brain hadn't had a chance to process it. The dragon was nowhere to be seen. The man stirred slightly, bringing my attention back to him and making my heart thump so loudly, I was sure he'd hear it.

"Hello," I called out hesitantly.

He lifted his head and ran his eyes from the tips of my toes all the way to my now disheveled hair. He looked tired, exhausted even, but it was his eyes that threw me, piercing green and staring right at me. It was unnerving.

55

I unhooked my armor with blundering fingers and pulled my tunic over my head, leaving me in just my vest and leggings. It wasn't ideal but it was better than the alternative. I took a few tentative steps towards the strange man, holding my tunic in front of me.

"Did the dragon bring you up here too?" I asked nervously. Those eyes!

He took my tunic but his eyes narrowed as an expression of intense confusion crossed his face. A wrinkle appeared on his forehead as he studied me. I had an overwhelming feeling that I'd done something wrong. It didn't help that he still hadn't covered himself.

"The tunic is for you," I said, gesturing at the garment. "It's cold up here." He still appeared confused as he pulled my tunic over his head. It was entirely too small for him, the green material stretching over every muscle on his torso. At least it covered him although it would do little against the cold. I shivered slightly, feeling it myself.

"You didn't see me?" he asked. His voice was deep and warm like molasses.

"Not at first. The dragon must have been blocking you. I don't know how we're going to get out of this."

He smiled then, dimples appearing on his cheek. His stunning green eyes, framed by the longest black eyelashes I'd ever seen, crinkled at the edges. If he wasn't so utterly beautiful, I'd have felt affronted by his lack of fear and obvious humor at our situation.

"Come with me," he said.

He walked past me, affording me a generous look at his tunic-covered behind and disappeared into the cave directly behind us.

I stood still, rooted to the spot. Did he really want me to follow him? What exactly did he expect to find in the cave? I suspected there to be nothing more than the bones of animals and quite possibly those of the occasional human. This dragon obviously liked to play with its food before eating it.

He stuck his head out of the mouth of the cave.

"Are you coming or not? I can assure you there is no other way out of here."

I threw my armor back on haphazardly, picked up my sword and followed him. What other choice did I have?

The cave was a lot deeper than I had expected and surprisingly devoid of bones. A pile of clothes lay by the mouth of the cave and it was these that the man went to. Without any embarrassment, he pulled my tunic off, throwing it to me before pulling on the pants and top that had been left there. What the hell was going on? There was no way it was a coincidence that those clothes were there.

"Who are you? What's happening?" I probably should have felt more scared than I did. Maybe I was in shock?

He came toward me with something in his hands. It was only when he wrapped it around me that I realized it was a coat. Thick fur-lined the inside, warming me instantly and almost pulling me down with its weight.

"The coat if for you. It's cold up here." He smiled at me again and pulled the coat tighter around me, my heart flipping at his closeness. If I stood on the very tip of my toes, I'd be eye to eye with him, but as it was I had to look up to meet his gaze. A thick mop of messy black hair that was way overdue for a haircut sat atop his head, giving him a raw, feral look. His clothes, although perfectly suited to the altitude, were messily sewn together and had almost certainly never seen a sewing pattern. Unlike my own; our seamstresses were very dedicated to their skill.

For the briefest of seconds, I wondered if I'd inadvertently been dropped into his home and he actually lived in the cave before brushing the ridiculous idea aside. He was thoughtful in a way no cave dweller would be and he had manners.

Although a little voice inside reminded me that he'd shown no discomfort in being completely naked around a stranger.

"Follow me," he said, beckoning me towards the back of the cave which was completely black.

"What if the dragon is back there?" I asked, wondering if I hadn't just jumped from the frying pan into the fat.

"The dragon will not harm you." He laughed and headed towards the dark. I waited until it had swallowed him whole before making a decision. On one hand, I could walk into what was almost certainly a dragon's lair with a complete stranger who I'd already seen naked; or on the other, I could go sit on the ledge outside and wait to die of frostbite or starvation. What a choice.

"Wait!" I called out. "I can't see you."

He stepped back into the light. "I'm sorry. I forgot that your eyesight won't be as good as mine."

"My eyesight is perfectly normal, thank you!" I replied haughtily, making him laugh at me once again. What was it with this man?

"Forgive me. I only meant that you might not be able to see as well in the dark as I can. Let me help you." He held out his hand in such a way it was obvious he wanted me to take it. Part of me wanted to tell him to stick it but another part didn't want to be left alone on a freezing cold ledge hundreds of feet above the ground. I was completely ignoring the much larger part of me that wanted to touch him so badly, to feel the warmth of his skin.

Just thinking about it caused my cheeks to redden. The heat rising into my face made my mind up for me. Maybe going into the dark cave where he couldn't see just how much he'd affected me wasn't the worst idea after all.

I took his hand and let him lead me into the darkness. He was much warmer than he had any right to be after being naked in these freezing temperatures. His hands were softer than I had imagined they would be and that source of heat was both comforting and thrilling at the same time. The whole thing was confusing—the insane condition I had found myself in and the feelings the situation was generating inside me. I was probably in shock. Perhaps riding a dragon could do that to a person.

"Something tells me you know something I don't," I said, feeling my way along a narrow tunnel. The ground was rocky beneath my feet and the going was slow. How he was managing with no shoes on was beyond me.

"Very astute," he replied, infuriating me further. I stumbled on a rock, tightening my grip on his hand to stop myself from falling. The walls of the tunnel were damp back here. My hand dragged against the side of the cave and the water accumulating there.

"You know where you're going, don't you? Those clothes weren't there coincidentally."

"That's right."

I could actually feel him smiling. I couldn't see him at all but I knew the corners of his mouth were turned upwards. He was having fun at my expense.

"Are you going to enlighten me?" I queried.

"What do you want to know?"

"Who are you?" I figured we'd start with the basics. I'd get on to the whole question of why he was naked on a ledge later.

"My name is Ash."

"I'm Julianna," I said, then paused. "Is that all? Are you going to tell me where you come from?"

"My people live up here on the mountain."

I laughed, thinking he was telling a joke, but his silence told me he wasn't.

"You're serious? No one lives on these mountains. The terrain is too difficult to climb.

There's no possible way to get back to the village from here without falling to your death."

"Who said anything about going to your village?"

"But how do you get food without going down the mountain? It's too cold to grow anything up here."

"You'll see," he replied. "Look, there's light ahead."

And he was right. The cave wasn't a cave at all but a tunnel through the mountain. As it grew lighter, the less I needed his help. I could see well enough to navigate the rough ground beneath me but I was reluctant to let go of his hand. He didn't seem in any hurry to let go of mine either.

We emerged on another ledge with no way down. Below, a lush, verdant valley spread out into the distance, surrounded by snowy peaks. A tiny town hundreds of feet below us looked like a toy village from this height. The view took my breath away. It was like nowhere I'd ever seen before and not in a million years would I have guessed that the aged Triad Mountains would hide such a utopia.

"It's...it's...stunning!"

"It's home," he replied simply, shrugging his shoulders.

As I gazed in wonder at the spectacular view below me, it dawned on me that two tiny dots on the horizon I'd taken as birds were in fact dragons.

"Don't you have a lot of problems with dragons up here?" I wondered aloud, glad that they were so far away.

"Much more than you could imagine," he smiled again.

"There's no path down the mountain," I pointed out. The cliffs were as sheer on this side as they were on the other. "How are we supposed to get down there?"

"You really haven't figured it out yet?" he asked, amusement filling his voice. He pulled his shirt over his shoulders, exposing his muscled chest, before moving to his belt.

"Hey, hey," I shouted, taking a step back in alarm. The ground crumbled beneath my feet and I could feel myself begin to fall.

A pair of strong hands caught hold of the coat's collar and pulled me away from the edge.

"You need to be careful."

"I need to be careful?" I shouted, my heart hammering at my near death fall into the valley. "What do you think you're doing?"

"Oh God, I'm sorry." He pulled away from me and sat at the mouth of the tunnel on a smooth boulder, his head in his hands. "I sometimes forget. We're so isolated up here that I didn't realize how rude I was being."

"Darn right you were being rude. What is it with you and having no clothes on?"

"I promise, I wasn't trying to scare or offend you," he said looking at me, contrition filling his features.

I didn't know what to think. He was acting so strangely and yet I could see that he was genuinely upset at scaring me.

"I have to take my clothes off to get us down the mountain."

"I really don't see the connection between the two."

For the life of me, I had no idea what he was trying to tell me. Not unless he had a plan to build a makeshift parachute out of his pants.

"I can't change with my clothes on. They'd rip to shreds."

"Change? Change into what?"

"Those dragons over there? They're my family, Julianna. I'm the dragon that brought you here."

CHAPTER SIX

ou're what?" I looked at him uncertainly.

"We are an ancient colony of dragons. We're shifters."

"The dragons are humans?" I asked incredulously.

"Not quite, no. We have a human form, that is true, but we do not identify as such. Nor do we really identify as full dragons. We are somewhere in between and happy to be that way. We keep to ourselves and only ever come down the mountain when absolutely necessary."

"But I'm a dragon slayer," I muttered, feeling a mixture of confusion and intrigue, not to mention a healthy dose of guilt about my own ancestry.

"Are you?" He looked at me with such warmth that my guilt began to melt away. "Julianna, I've lived up on these mountains my whole life and I've been brought up on stories of our enemies, the men and women of your village who call themselves dragon slayers, but not once have I known anyone to do what you did today."

"What did I do?"

"You hesitated. You could have killed me but you didn't. You actually risked your own life because deep down you really didn't want to harm me, did you?" The warmth in his eyes made me feel unsure of myself.

"I thought you were a mother dragon. I saw the egg and thought it was cruel to take a mother away from her baby."

He laughed which only added to my confusion. "The egg is a decoy—polished rock in a fake nest. It's been there as long as I can remember. As you can see below us, we live in houses, much the same as you do."

"But why?"

"I guess it was put there in a misguided attempt to ward the slayers off." He shrugged. "We hoped that your people would leave us alone if you thought we had babies to look after. Of course, the opposite happened. They saw that we were breeding and stepped up the amount of people coming here."

"I didn't know," I said, feeling ashamed.

"I know you didn't, but you're the first of your kind to think before mindlessly killing us. I'm going to give you two choices, Julianna. There is no way off this mountain without wings. I will happily transform back and take you home, or at least to a place that will be safe for you to get home."

"I want the second choice!" I butted in.

His mouth curled up at the edges as he regarded me. "I've only given you one choice so far."

"You were going to invite me to your village." As soon as I said it, I hoped I was right. Now that I knew it existed, I knew I wasn't ready to go home and forget its existence.

He chuckled. "You're a mind reader, no? I was indeed going to offer to let you come to my homeland but I must warn you, if that is what you choose, it will not be without risks. My people are fiercely proud and much like your people, we have a deep-rooted fear and dislike of outsiders."

"So why were you going to invite me?"

"Because fear is brought about by misunderstanding. War could so easily be avoided if the two parties communicated."

"Is this war?" I asked.

"Isn't it?"

I looked over the pretty little village hundreds of feet below us. I wondered for a second what my father would make of it.

"I'm going to have to strip again. You might want to cover your eyes."

Despite my fear of heights, I walked to the edge and sat, dangling my feet over. The village looked tiny from here, not scary at all as long as I didn't think of the fact that it was full of dragons, or dragon people. Dragon people who had spent centuries being hunted by my people.

I tried to ignore the sickening sounds coming from behind me. Shifting sounded really painful. I'd heard of shifters before but they were creatures in distant lands and were spoken about in almost mythical terms. It was difficult to imagine a whole colony of them so close to where I lived. My shoulder suddenly got very warm as a blast of fire flew over me. I turned to see a dragon waiting for me to climb aboard his back.

Climbing up was trickier than I had imagined. He was just so big. He lifted his leg for me to use as a step and I grabbed the base of his wing to pull myself aboard. It felt much weirder sitting on top of him now that I knew what he really was. The discarded pile of clothes only served to make me more uncomfortable.

Flinging my arms around his neck as we took off, I held on tightly for fear of falling. The wind blew around me sending my hair flying out behind me. It was so strong that I could barely keep my eyes open, but I did, just so I could enjoy the magnificent sight. Adrenaline pumped through my system as Ash circled high above the village, giving me a bird's eye view.

"Woohoo!" I shouted as he did a steep dive before pulling back up straight moments later. The thrill of flying was like nothing I had ever felt before, not even close. Blood rushed through my veins and my heart pounding in a mixture of fear and utter excitement. I had never felt as free as I did now, soaring high in the air.

All too soon, my thrill ride ended and we came to a gentle landing on the very edge of the village. Another neatly folded pile of clothes greeted us, ready for his return. I jumped down and ran towards a fence at the edge of a neatly tilled field while he changed into his human form and dressed. I was eager for him to finish so I could tell him how wonderful the flight down had been, how exhilarating. I peeped around to find him buttoning the top two buttons on his shirt.

"Oh my goodness. That was amazing!" I jumped up and down making him laugh. "I flew, Ash. I really flew."

I knew I sounded dorky but I didn't care. I felt high as a kite. I might have touched down but I was still flying.

"Yes, you did. Did you enjoy the dip I did for you?"

"Next time can we do a loop-the-loop?" I held my hands together almost pleadingly.

"I know I could but you'd probably plummet to your death. Maybe we should put that idea on a back burner for now. Come on, I'll introduce you to Spear, our leader."

"Okay," I said, full of excitement.

"Before I take you into the village, I have to warn you. Spear does not like slayers, with much reason. His mother was killed by one. He makes sure our village is defended from your kind and he will not take well to me bringing you here."

My excitement swiftly turned to fear.

"He will not hurt you; he is a proud man and he is angry with your people, but he is not a bad man."

"Are you sure?" He must be pretty livid if we slayed his mother, not that I could really blame him. I would be too.

"You'll be safe with me, come on." He took my hand again, just as he had done in the caves. The warmth of his skin reassured me as we walked past fenced fields. The houses were built in a similar way to ours although they were much closer together. Each house had a flat roof, unlike the ones in my own village which were sloping.

I wondered why for a second before I saw a dragon land on the top of one of them. They were landing spots. Despite the fact I knew the dragons were really people, I still shied away from the one on the roof. Years of having it instilled in me that dragons were killers was enough to make me wary and afraid. Even Ash's warm hand was not enough to stop the fear running through me.

The houses became denser as we got closer to the center of the village, and more and more commercial buildings appeared. I was surprised to see shops although I didn't know why. Unlike the shops in my world, everything they sold seemed to come from this small valley—grains and vegetables from the fields, a butcher's shop selling beef and pork, a basic clothes shop selling handwoven attire. All the buildings were made out of wood.

"That's our town hall," Ash said, pointing out a circular building ahead of us. It was thatched with straw which I couldn't help but think was a fire hazard with all the dragons around. Ash gripped my hand more firmly as we entered through a set of double doors.

I found myself in a curved corridor, more than likely circling the entire building. Posters of events and news from around the village were pinned up on the walls haphazardly. Instead of turning left or right, we walked through another set of doors ahead of us, bringing us out into a huge circular courtyard with strange holes evenly distributed around the edge. One side was raised slightly like a stage although there were no chairs. Ash guided me forward and slightly to the right where there was a set of stairs leading down into the ground. At the bottom was a heavy wooden door which Ash pulled back easily, despite the fact it looked extraordinarily heavy.

The room we walked into was the strangest room I'd ever seen. Unlike the building above, this was made entirely of stone although it had some handwoven rugs on the floor to give it the appearance of being homely. The use of the holes above suddenly became apparent—they were windows to let light into this strange room. It looked very much like a courtroom that we would have back home with a raised podium at one side and rows of wooden benches at the other. Behind the podium was a door which was where Ash led me. This time, instead of just entering, he knocked and waited.

I shivered slightly, partly because of the cold, mainly out of nerves.

"Maybe I should go home," I whispered. "This is a mistake."

"Come in," a deep voice boomed.

"You'll be fine," he replied warmly and opened the door.

"Ash, what are you doing?" asked a great big man sitting behind a long desk. He looked to be in his early forties although his black hair was graying slightly at the sides. His voice was even and calm and his face showed no emotion but his eyes flashed with anger. Anger at me.

"Hear me out, Spear. She doesn't want to kill us."

"Of course, she wants to kill us," he replied as if I wasn't standing before him. "She is one of them." He spat the last word out as if he was talking about vermin.

"She had the chance to kill me and she didn't. Even with all her men behind her, she chose to spare me."

"Ash!" Spear stood up and slammed his fist on the table. The resulting boom echoed around the room, making me jump in fright. "I don't care what she did or didn't do. She is a slayer. For centuries, her people have been killing ours. That's all they know how to do. She's no different. She will need to be killed now that she knows where we live.

"I didn't want to kill him. I don't want to kill anybody," I replied nervously, trying to ignore his last statement.

"Nobody needs to be killed. That's exactly why I brought her here. To see who we are. To give her a chance."

"Are you suggesting we just let her go free? Within days there will be swarms of slayers up here and we will all be dead."

"You know as well as I do that there is no way they can get up this high on the mountain. We're perfectly safe up here."

"I've heard rumors of flying machines built in distant lands. If they know we're here, it's only a matter of time before the slayers figure out a way to get up here. I'm sorry, Ash, but she has to be disposed of. We cannot trust her to keep our colony a secret."

"I will!" I shouted before I'd even thought about what I was saying. As a slayer, could I really promise anything of the sort?

"She has said she will keep out secret and I believe her. You can't make decisions as big as this without the rest of the village elders anyway. There has to be a majority vote."

Spear's eyebrows scrunched as defeat reflected in his eyes. I took a deep breath as I realized that there was a chance of surviving this after all.

"It will take a week to gather everyone," Ash continued. "There are still a couple of scouting parties out over the eastern rim. Let her stay here and get to know everyone before just deciding she must die. Let her prove she means no harm."

"I don't like it but protocol must be maintained. If she proves that she can be trusted and the Elders believe her then I am powerless; however, if, like me, they pass the death sentence, then she will have to die. I'm putting you in charge of her, Ash, and if I hear about her putting just a toe out of line, it will not only be her head on the chopping block. Do you understand?"

"Completely. You have my word, I'll look after her."

"As well you might. She is as unsafe here as we are in her world. With any luck, I won't have to bring this to the elders in a week. I'll be surprised if she lives that long."

He went back to his writing as Ash and I left the room. My nerves, already frayed from everything else that had happened that day, were now on a knife edge.

"He's all bark and no bite," said Ash in an attempt to reassure me. It didn't work.

"No bite? He just sentenced me to death!"

"The elders won't allow it. Once they meet you and get to know you, they'll know that you're telling the truth. I know that you won't tell your family about us; we just have to prove it to them."

I gulped. I'd only said what I'd said because I was faced with certain death otherwise. If I never spoke of this place, it would be a massive betrayal to my family. Was I really able to do that? I wasn't even sure myself.

"Where are we going?" I asked Ash as we left the circular building and headed down a street I'd not previously seen.

"I'm taking you home."

Ash's hand squeezed mine and I suddenly realized that he'd not let go of my hand the whole time.

CHAPTER SEVEN

e headed back toward the cliffs we had flown down from, but this time proceeded much further along.

"Do you live in a house on the outskirts of town?" I asked as the houses once again thinned out to be replaced by more of the farmed land.

"Kind of," he replied mysteriously. We passed a field full of cows munching lazily on grass.

There was only one house I could see now—a pretty little cottage with a thatched roof and smoke drifting out of the chimney. It was here I thought we were headed but we walked past it.

"There are no houses left," I exclaimed as we left the cottage behind.

"Look ahead of you."

I looked towards the cliffs and that's when I noticed a series of caves in the sheer rock. There were lots of them, maybe fifty or sixty, but unlike normal caves, they were uniform in the rock and each had a doorway or window intricately carved with effigies of dragons. There was no way these were natural. Someone had spent years lovingly carving homes out of the hillside. Ten of the holes were at ground level and had wooden doors on them. The rest were windows, some with balconies. They stretched quite a way up the cliff, showing the immense size of each dwelling.

We arrived at a periwinkle blue door that Ash pushed open. A huge, gangly dog came running up to him, its long ears flopping behind it. It jumped up and began to lick Ash as if he had been away for months.

"Hey, Firecracker," Ash said, giving the dog a friendly ruffle of its hair.

It surprised me that a dragon would have a pet dog. A lot of things were surprising me today. The dog finally put its two front paws back on the ground and came to give me a sniff.

"He's very cute." I grinned, patting him on the head.

"She. She's a girl. Come on, I'd like you to meet my mom."

I hesitated. I felt comfortable around Ash but Spear had scared me. What if Ash's mom felt the same way about me that Spear had?

The entrance hall was the strangest place I'd ever seen. The walls were roughly hewn out of the rock but the floor was polished wood. Framed pictures of unknown people lined the walls and coats hung on a row of hooks. A mirror hung next to where I stood, a shelf below it. A couple of unlit candles sat on an old table, waiting to be lit.

I hazarded a glance in the mirror. My hair had settled into a frizzy mess and I was covered in dirt. When I pulled Ash's coat from my shoulders, I realized I looked like a warrior with my armor still on over my clothes.

Straight ahead was another door and to the right of that, stairs leading up to the next level.

"My mom will be in the living area, come on."

He seemed eager to take me to his mom, but I couldn't possibly meet her looking the way I did.

"Do you have a bathroom I can use first?"

"Sure. That door over there is a guest toilet."

I opened the door expecting to find a hole in the ground but was quite surprised to find a true bathroom with a little sink and another mirror. Water poured out of a little channel and streamed into the rock basin where it gurgled down a hole in the middle. The water was freezing but it refreshed me as I splashed it over my face. I did my best to tame my hair with the few pins that had survived the journey and then pulled off all my armor. I wanted to meet Ash's mom as an equal, not as a slayer. My tunic was filthy but it would have to do.

Looking in the mirror, I tried to imagine what Ash's mom would think of me. Did I look like a slayer? I didn't think so, not now that I had taken my armor off, but I hardly looked like a lady either. I was just about to tell Ash to forget the whole thing when he knocked on the door.

"Are you okay? You've been in there a long time."

"I'll be right out."

Steeling myself, I opened the door and followed Ash to a landing with two doors. The stairs continued up to another level but it was the first door that Ash opened. Just like the hallway, this room had been cut out of the mountain. The walls were nothing more than jagged edges of rock but there was carpet on the floor and family paintings hanging alongside landscapes. Whoever had painted them was quite an artist. The room was also a lot lighter than I imagined it would be thanks to a large window at one end. At the other end of the room was a table with four chairs. An elegant lady with her hair in a long braid down her back sat at one of these.

"Hi, Mom. I've got someone I'd like you to meet."

She looked up with a beautiful smile on her face but when she saw me her face dropped.

"Ash, who is this?" she asked although I could tell from her expression and the tone of her voice she already knew what I was, if not who.

"This is Julianna. She's—"

"No!" said his mother, cutting him off mid-sentence.

"No, what?" asked Ash but he knew what she meant. We both did.

"Maybe you should just take me home," I said quietly. It was obvious I wasn't wanted here.

"No!" replied Ash. "Mom, I want her to stay with us. This is what we've been talking about for years. You've said it yourself a million times how you wished things didn't have to be as they are. Well, now is our chance to make that happen."

"I didn't mean invite one into our home. I'm sorry, Julianna, is it? I have nothing against you personally although what Ash was thinking by bringing you here is beyond me. But you will have hardship here." She turned back to Ash. "If Spear catches her with you, we'll all be in trouble. Take her home quickly before he finds out what you've done."

"He already knows. I took her to meet him first."

"Spear knows? I'm surprised she's still here to tell the tale."

"He wants to put her to death but he's giving her a week to prove her loyalty to us."

"Ash, she has no loyalty to us and why should she? I'm surprised at you after what happened to your father."

"That was nothing to do with Julianna and you know that. She had the chance to kill me today and she chose not to. All slayers are not what we have painted them to be. What if we have been wrong all these years?"

"Hundreds of our people slain over the centuries tell a different story, Ash."

"If Julianna hesitated, why wouldn't there be others who would also spare us? I'm only asking for her to be here a week. Spear told me I have to look after her. After that, if she has not persuaded enough of our villagers that she's loyal to us, then I'll take her to Spear myself."

"If that is what Spear has said then we cannot go against it, but it will be for one week only, Ash. She can have the top bedroom. I'll bring her some clean bedding later."

"Thank you, Mom," said Ash, crossing the room to kiss her cheek.

"Thank you, Mrs.—" I paused, not knowing what to call her.

"Edeline." Her eyes met Ash's for a brief second before turning to me. "If you're to live among my family, you may as well know my first name."

"Thank you, Edeline."

"I have no fight with you child, but you must know that being here among us will not be easy. People here hold grudges. Ash, show her to the top bedroom." She sighed as she turned from us and disappeared down the hall.

"Yes, Mom."

I followed Ash through the overly wide doorway and up the stairs which wound back on themselves. We passed at least three floors before the stairway opened into a large room. The walls were smoother up here and blackened by fire but there were none of the home furnishings of downstairs. The whole room was empty save for a mound of straw.

"I'm sorry, it's not very homely. We don't normally use this room as a bedroom. I guess you can say we don't have many overnight guests." Ash shrugged his shoulders. "We use it to fly in. Our landing pad is through those glass doors."

Opening the doors he motioned to, I stepped out onto the large terrace. The view over the village was stunning, even in the fading light, with verdant fields laid out below me and the houses of the village in the distance now lit up with twinkling lights.

"I could sleep up here and you can have my room if you prefer."

"I love it!"

"You do?" asked Ash as I followed him back into the room.

The hay looked dry and clean and was as good a place for me to sleep as any. It reminded me of our barn back home. I had fallen asleep there many nights, just gazing at the stars through the holes in the roof. If I ignored the faint burning smell, I could be comfortable here.

"I'll find a bed for you to sleep on and bring it up."

I bit my tongue, embarrassed that I had assumed they slept on hay, and thankful that I hadn't said as much.

"That's very kind of you. Thanks."

"It's beginning to get late. I'll get it now."

When he had gone, I stepped back out onto the terrace. The light was fading quickly. A whole day had passed since I'd jumped on Ash's back. I wondered where my father and Jasper were now. Would they still be out looking for me or would they have gone back to the village to tell my mother that I was gone?

Either of those options was enough to bring tears to my eyes. Ash had promised I'd be loyal to the dragons but was that something I could really do?

A few moments later, a clattering in the room behind me told me that Ash had arrived back with the bed. He'd brought it up in four pieces which he dropped on the floor.

"It just slots together. Do you think you can manage while I bring up the mattress?"

"I'll try."

In reality, having something physical to do took my thoughts away from the situation. I'd just slotted the last two bits together when Ash came back with the mattress and a huge fabric bag, out of which he produced blankets and a pillow. Following that, he pulled a loaf of bread and some butter.

My stomach gurgled at the sight. I'd not had a bite to eat since my mother made me breakfast that morning.

"It's not much, sorry. It's all we had." He chuckled quietly. "We hunt most of our food."

"It looks delicious." I eyed the bread still sitting in his hand.

We both sat on the newly made bed and Ash ripped chunks from the bread and dipped them in the warmed butter. I couldn't help but smile at the thought of my mother's face if she ever saw anyone eating like that. She was the type of person that cut the crusts off her sandwiches.

Ash handed me the first chunk, gooey with butter. I bit down on it and let the liquid butter ooze down my throat.

I don't know if it was because I hadn't eaten all day or because it felt naughty to be eating in such a savage manner, but it tasted utterly delicious. We devoured the whole loaf between us and drank a bottle of milk that Ash had also brought out of the bag.

I felt completely at ease but something that Edeline had said was gnawing at me.

"Ash?"

"Hmmm?" he responded around a mouth full of bread.

"What did your mother mean earlier? What happened to your father?"

He chewed thoughtfully before swallowing the bread and turning his eyes to me. I could see the pain in them but there was no malice.

"My father was killed by a slayer last year."

The way he looked at me was enough to break my heart. It took everything I had not to reach out to him, but how could I? One of my kind killed his father. Who was I to offer sympathy?

"I should leave you now. It's getting late," said Ash, standing and putting the empty bottle back in the now depleted bag. "Will you be okay?"

I nodded my head numbly, not knowing what to say to him. He was acting as though nothing had happened, as if everything was okay.

"Ash," I called out as he was leaving the room.

He turned to me and nodded slightly. It was his way of telling me that he didn't blame me. He closed the door, leaving me alone with my thoughts.

I laid my head back on the surprisingly comfortable mattress and pulled the blanket over me. The only light in the room came from the glow of the town through the window. Strange sounds filtered from the outside, although it was so much quieter than I was used to. I heard shuffling from someone moving about downstairs and hushed voices although they were far too faint to tell who they belonged to.

My mind flew to my father and Jasper searching for me, the thought of them making me homesick even though I'd only been away for a day. No one had ever gone up to the mountains and not returned before. Some had been unsuccessful in slaying a dragon, but we had never had one of the villagers go missing. I wondered if they thought I was dead. Even if they still hoped I was alive, they would never be able to reach me—not this high up.

I closed my eyes and thought of Ash. How could he be so nice to me when one of my kind had murdered his father? I had felt no blame from him but my guilt was palpable. More than anything, I wanted to make it up to him, but how? I closed my eyes and shivered even though the room was warm. Thoughts turned into dreams which turned into nightmares of dragons and fire, and by the time I woke up, I still felt conflicted about my feelings towards Ash and the situation I had found myself in.

Chapter Eight

The smell of something cooking wafted up the stairs and woke me from my bad dreams. It was definitely some kind of meat and smelled delicious. My stomach gave a gurgle to concur. I followed the smell downstairs, expecting to find Ash or Edeline cooking. I searched the whole house, calling out their names but no one answered. I saw no sign of the sister that Ash mentioned, nor Firecracker.

As I searched from room to room, it became apparent that they did not own a kitchen and yet the smell of food was stronger down here. It was only when I got to the bottom floor and the entrance hall that I heard the sound of people outside. I opened the door hesitantly to find a large group of people sitting around a huge fire pit. Flames licked a grill that had been laid on top and filled with great slabs of meat.

"Here she is!" Ash stood up from the circle of people and walked towards me. Two dozen eyes swiveled my way, making me feel more nervous today than I had yesterday. I also spotted Edeline in the group and a young girl sitting beside her that must have been Ash's sister.

Firecracker bounded over, passing Ash and licking my fingers. I gave him a pat on the head for his troubles.

"Come. There are some people I would like you to meet." Ash held out his hand for me to take but I was reluctant to do so. I could see the expressions on some faces and they weren't happy.

"They know about you. I've already told them. You'll be fine," Ash said in an effort to comfort me. I held out my hand to his reluctantly but when our fingers touched, I suddenly felt safe. It was as if nothing could hurt me when Ash was at my side.

I walked with him to the group of people. There was a pretty even split between women and men, of young and old and of those smiling at me and those grimacing at my presence. Not that I could blame them.

"Everybody, this is Julianna."

I gave a shy smile and waved. An elderly man to my right patted the rock beside him to indicate that I could sit there. I let go of Ash's hand and took the offered seat so as not to cause offense. The young girl came over to me carrying a plate with a huge steak on it and handed it to me, grinning. She looked to be about twelve years old with burnished red hair in short braids at either side. Her coloring was different from the dark-haired Ash, but her cheeky face was the spitting image of her elder brother's.

"What's it like over there? I've never been over the mountain. I'm too young but I can't wait until I'm big enough to fly there. Do you have rivers? Ash told me that the roads are made of gold."

She was a whirlwind but I immediately liked her.

"We have rivers," I laughed. "But we have roads much like yours. Very few of us have any gold. Only the richest people of our village own any and they make it into jewelry."

"Wow!" Her eyes rounded like saucers. "I'd love some gold jewelry. I only have this." She showed me a polished rock threaded through a bit of string that hung around her neck.

"Maybe one day I could give you one of my brooches. I have a couple of gold ones."

She jumped up and hugged me, nearly causing me to drop my plate. "I'm so glad you brought her here, Ash," she squealed before letting me go.

"Yes, that's right, give her some gold," sneered a voice from the other side of the fire pit. "That's really going to make up for you murdering her father."

I looked through the flames to a very good-looking man with blonde hair. Even sitting down, he was obviously tall. His shoulders were wide, topping off muscular arms and I could see the outline of his muscles under his tunic. His nose was scrunched as his eyes tracked me.

I had just opened my mouth to reply when I felt my arm being pulled up by Ash. I rose to my feet in surprise, knocking the steak to the ground. Firecracker ran over to my feet and picked it up between her teeth.

"Stop it, Aluss. I warned you not to talk to her in such a way."

He stood up, his huge size almost blocking the light from the sun. He was at least a head taller than Ash and three times wider. I'd never seen someone so huge and so strong. "Yeah, you warned me, but what exactly are you going to do to stop me?"

Fear gripped me as Ash skirted around the campfire, pulling me closer to the brute.

"I'm not fighting you. We need to stop this ridiculous war once and for all. Killing ourselves is only going to make the slayers' jobs easier, don't you think? Now get out of our way. I'm going to show Julianna around the village. I was hoping we would show her how welcoming we can be but thanks to you, you've only cemented her assumption that we're all savages."

"He's got every right to voice his opinion. We're all thinking the same thing." The speaker was a woman about my age who would have been attractive was it not for the way hatred twisted her features.

"What is wrong with you all? Julianna hasn't done anything to you, Lisa, or you, Aluss. You weren't out there yesterday. I was. I saw what she's like. She chose to risk her life to save mine. They're not all bad people on the other side of the mountain."

"You are such a fool, Ash," replied Lisa. "She didn't kill you then so she could find out where we live and bring her family back to slaughter us all. You're such a sucker for a pretty face."

"You're wrong!" Ash's hand tightened around mine. "Come on, Julianna."

I had no choice but to follow him and leave the others behind. He took me along the same track we'd walked down the previous day, moving at such a pace he was almost dragging me.

"Wait up!" I said, barely able to keep up with him.

"Sorry!" He turned and kicked a rock behind us. "I'm just so angry. They knew you were going to join us and they treated you like that anyway."

"How can you expect them to treat me any differently? I'm more surprised at the way you treat me."

"What do you mean?" His eyes softened as he looked towards me. There was a hint of something in them, not fear exactly, but worry.

"My people killed your father and countless others and yet you treat me with such warmth. I don't understand it."

I saw him glance behind me to see if there was anyone in earshot.

"I want you to understand that I don't blame you for the death of my father."

"The others do."

"Aluss looks mean but really he's just stupid. He's all brawn and no brain. He likes to flex his muscles and throw his weight around but you've nothing to fear from him."

"What about Lisa?" From nowhere a surge of jealousy rose up within me. It was as though just saying her name gave her some connection to Ash. I couldn't even begin to fathom why I cared, but I knew that I did. I almost didn't want to hear what he was about to say.

"Lisa was my girlfriend."

"Was?" I knew it was none of my business but I couldn't keep myself from asking.

"We dated a while last year. She cheated on me with Aluss."

"Oh," I said, not knowing how to respond. I couldn't deny that a feeling of relief rushed through me, as undeniable and as strange as the jealousy I had felt moments before.

We walked in silence around the perimeter of the little village. Once on the other side, the terrain was more rugged than the farmland. Soft rolling hills covered by the greenest grass and hundreds of pretty pink and red flowers made a valley for the clearest stream I'd ever seen to wind through.

We crossed the stream, stepping on flat stones that had been placed there for that very reason. As we strolled up the low hill, a couple of dragons took off by the cliffs, a large gold one followed by a smaller green one. They flew closer to us, getting larger as they soared above our heads.

"That's Aluss and Lisa," said Ash

"Where are they going?" I squinted into the sun as they disappeared over the cliffs at the opposite side.

"To hunt," he replied, sitting on the soft grass. I followed his lead and sat beside him, trying not to flatten any of the flowers as I did.

I gazed out over the village, seeing the farmland in the distance.

"You have cows and pigs. Why do you need to hunt?"

"We do farm, but it's not enough for us. You've seen the size of us when we are dragons. It takes an inordinate amount of energy for us to change forms. We have huge appetites. Most of the food we eat is hunted. Aluss and Lisa will bring home a few goats between them, or maybe if we're lucky, a couple of the wild buffalo that live on the plains on the other side. After lunch, another group will go out hunting and we'll eat whatever they bring back for our dinner."

"There are a lot of you and you so easily outnumber the people in my village. Why don't you...?"

"Why don't we kill your people?" He finished the question so that I didn't have to. The shame I felt was so overwhelming that I couldn't look at him. Instead, I gazed at the broken stem of a flower on the ground near my feet—anything to stop me having to raise my eyes to his.

"My people do not kill. We hunt for food but we do not hunt out of malice. You and I are the same really. Yes, I have the power to turn into a dragon but that doesn't make me a savage beast."

"I don't think you're a savage beast," I said, flashing my eyes towards him to find almost a smile on his face.

"But yesterday you did."

"Yesterday I didn't know you."

"And therein lies the solution." He picked a flower and handed it to me, taking me by surprise.

"Thank you," I replied, taking the flower from him. It was one of the red ones, with a long stem and six perfectly shaped petals. I didn't have to bring it to my nose to smell it; the whole field was filled with the fragrance of these flowers. Nothing remotely like them grew on our side of the cliffs. "These flowers are so beautiful. They're perfect in every way."

Ash just smiled which made me blush. It occurred to me that this was the first time in my life that a boy had given me flowers. I turned my head away to hide the color in my cheeks and went back to the conversation we'd been having before he'd handed the flower to me.

"What do you mean by solution?"

"It's easy to kill someone when you don't know them. Even easier when you believe them to be dangerous, and yet hand a man a sword to kill an equal, someone they know, and the job is a much harder one. You wouldn't kill me now because you've taken the time to get to know me."

"I didn't want to kill you yesterday when I didn't know you at all."

"Ah, but you are like that flower in your hand."

I could feel the blush deepen in my cheeks at his words. I'd called the flower beautiful. Was he saying the same about me?

He lay back on the carpet of grass, his hands behind his head. I followed his lead and lay back next to him, gazing up into the pale blue sky and enjoying the heat of the sun on my face. A small dragon with a yellow belly flew overhead.

"What do you see?" asked Ash as the dragon soared across the sky above us.

"I see a dragon."

"Yesterday it was a dragon. What are you seeing now?"

I looked at the dragon once more, tilting my head to follow its path. Above its belly, its skin was a dark red. Something about it caught in my consciousness. I'd seen that color already today.

"I think it's your sister."

"Lucy. Yes, it is. She likes you. When I told her last night that a villager from the other side of the cliffs was staying with us, she was so excited I had to order her not to go barging into your room. She's been begging to be allowed to fly over the cliffs since she first learned to talk, but she's too young. It's dangerous for her over there."

I thought back to the whirlwind of red hair and the exuberant little girl I'd met only a couple of hours before. She was so sweet and full of life. Would the slayers really have killed her? With a heavy heart, I knew that we would. We'd had smaller dragons brought to our village before. Why hadn't it occurred to anyone that these smaller dragons were nothing more than children?

"This needs to be stopped! Your sister should be free to fly wherever she wants without fear. We have to do something about this."

"That's why I brought you here. So you could see who we really are. Do you think you'll be able to convince your people that we are no threat?"

I looked back up into the sky as I pondered Ash's question. Lucy had disappeared from view. My father was a proud man and he was set in his ways. I'd been brought up a slayer, as had he and all the other villagers. However much I'd like to tell Ash yes, I wasn't sure if I could change centuries of hate, but as the small dragon flew back into view, I knew then that I'd do everything I could to try.

Chapter Nine

The sky darkened as a dragon blocked out the sun overhead.

"That's our cue, come on."

I sat up to see Aluss and Lisa pass overhead. Both had something in their mouths.

"Cue for what?" I rubbed my eyes and yawned. We'd spent the whole day lazing on the grassy hillside amongst the flowers, enjoying the sun and chatting effortlessly. It had been the most blissful way to while away the day and I didn't want it to end. Not just yet.

"Dinner. You must be hungry. You didn't even get breakfast this morning."

"Do we really have to go back now?" My time with Ash had been perfect and I wasn't sure if I was ready for it to end. I felt so comfortable around him. He listened when I talked about life on the other side of the cliffs without passing judgment, and he told me about his father and what a great man he'd been. Despite the fact that I was starving, going back to the other dragons meant I had to share his company and I wasn't ready for that. I liked having him all to myself. It felt as though going back amongst the other dragons would change everything although I couldn't quite put my finger on why.

Unfortunately, my stomach didn't have quite the same thoughts and betrayed me by gurgling loudly.

Ash jumped to his feet, holding his hand out to me. I'd held his hand before but after spending the day with him, it suddenly felt different. Before, he'd been either guiding me somewhere or offering support. This time it felt like something more. I took his hand and let him pull me to my feet, telling myself that he was only helping me up. It would have worked if he'd have let go once I was upright but he didn't. How was it possible for all my nerve endings to congregate in just one place? I had never been so aware of the palm of my hand before. His was warm and his touch made me feel safe but nervous. It was only as we walked back through the village that I realized he'd not given me the tour we'd set out to do in the first place.

In the distance, roaring flames lighted the cliff fronts in a warm orange glow. It caused me to pause.

"That's Aluss cooking the food," Ash said, gripping my hand tighter at my hesitation and pulling me forward.

The same group of dragons I'd seen this morning was sitting around the campfire. Even from a distance, I could sense an easy familiarity between them. It made me feel like even more of an outsider. Nerves took over as I recalled the way some of them had spoken to me this morning. I slowed my pace as we got close.

"I can't do this. I'm not really hungry."

Ash stopped and turned to me. "They're good people, really. Old prejudices die hard but that's why you need to stay strong."

111

"Their hatred towards me is understandable."

"They've been less than welcoming but they don't hate you. They just need to get used to you. I won't let them hurt you. I'll be there with you the whole time, right by your side."

My nerves dissipated slightly but I was still scared when we joined the circle. The chatting stopped and everything became silent as they all turned their eyes toward me.

Lisa threw me a look of pure loathing as I took a seat on one of the rocks, doing nothing to allay my fears. I gripped Ash's hand harder as he sat next to me.

Edeline walked toward me carrying a plate heaped with food. Whatever it was smelled delicious. Flame-cooked meat had never looked more appealing. There was also bread and salad on the plate she handed to me.

She addressed me while everyone watched. "I trust you had a good day?"

"We did. Thank you," I replied nervously. I felt like I was center stage with all eyes upon me, or like prey waiting to be devoured in the midst of hungry carnivores. Either way, it was disconcerting to have everyone looking at me, waiting for me to say or do something.

"I have an apology to make. We all do," began Edeline, loud enough for the whole group to hear. "Ash is very important to us and it has long been a dream of his to unite the dragon folk with the slayers so we could all come to understand one another and live in some kind of harmony. I must confess to thinking it a harmless daydream on his part and dismissed it as such. Yesterday, his dream became a plan when he brought you to us, and I for one felt uneasy about what it actually meant. We've all lived under the threat of your people for so long that they have become almost mythical. We've all suffered losses as a direct result of what your villagers have done and it has made us both angry and scared. However, we as a group have come to realize that if we treat you the way that we ourselves have been treated, then nothing can possibly change.

"Ash made it very clear that you had the chance to kill him and you made the decision not to. I

113

know of your custom of having the first kill on your eighteenth birthday and I understand how important it is to your people. It is a rite of passage. It must have taken great strength of character and compassion to choose to let Ash live, therefore we must offer the same compassion to you. We've all had a talk and we would officially like to welcome you to our land. You are a guest of Ash's and that makes you a guest of all of us."

I peeked around to see Ash beaming next to me. Edeline's speech had left me more than a little overwhelmed. I carefully placed the plate to my side and stood to give her a hug. Somewhere, someone in the circle began to clap and then one by one, everyone else joined in, first by clapping, then by stamping their feet in a cacophony of noise sounding like the center of a thunderstorm. When I let Edeline go and the noise had subsided, Aluss came up to me.

"I'm sorry about the way I treated you," he huffed. "I was wrong."

I gave him a shy smile and then, without thinking, gave him a quick peck on the cheek to which he grinned stupidly back at me. It was only when I sat back in my place that I noticed Lisa staring at me with such hatred that goosebumps sprouted on my arms and a shiver ran down my spine.

"See, I told you everything would be fine," whispered Ash, making me turn my eyes away from Lisa. I wasn't so sure. Okay, on the surface I had been accepted, but I still had Spear to worry about and the way Lisa looked at me told me that not everyone was so easy to forgive or to give others a chance.

The sound of music suddenly cut through the air and I looked up to find that some of the dragon people had started to play a lively jig by the side of the fire. Their instruments were completely alien to me—sets of wooden pipes, drums, and stringed instruments I had never seen before—but the music they played was joyous and fun and I couldn't help but tap my foot as I ate my dinner. Now that the awkwardness was over, the dinner had almost turned into a party. The elder dragons were drinking something that looked suspiciously like mead and the younger ones danced around to the music.

"Is this a special occasion?" I whispered to Ash who had already finished his food and was now clapping along to the beat.

"Just dinner. It's like this every night. Don't you have meals like this?" he asked, his eyes focused on the band.

The only times we ate like this was when we slayed a dragon but I could hardly tell him that. As I looked around at the group of people, it struck me how at ease they were together. Laughing, joking, eating and dancing as one family. The sense of easy cohesion and community between them made it very easy for me to have a sense of belonging. It felt wonderful but I knew that I didn't belong. These people were my sworn enemy, ingrained in me since birth, and thoughts of belonging to them were dangerous. And yet, when Lucy came to me and held out her hand for me to dance with her, I couldn't help but laugh and follow her onto the makeshift dance area that was really no more than a circle of well-worn dirt.

She giggled as I spun her around and around, under my arm and then both of us together. She loved every minute of it and if I was honest with myself, so did I.

"Can I have this dance?"

I stopped spinning Lucy to see Ash waiting patiently by my side. Lucy grinned and backed off to go sit with her mother. Dancing with Lucy had been effortless and a whole lot of fun. Why was it that the thought of dancing with Ash made my stomach turn to mush and my knees turn to jelly? He took my hand and spun me around in much the same way I had with Lucy except this time it was slower.

At some point, the music had changed from a festive jig to a slow dance. With his free hand, Ash grabbed my waist and pulled me close, leaving me no choice but to drape my free arm over his shoulder. The closeness between us was electrifying and terrifying at the same. I'd danced at slayer parties many times but never like this. I could barely breathe with excitement. The closeness of his body against mine scared me but made me feel both warm and safe, like being in the center of a hurricane of new emotions.

"Tomorrow is my day to hunt. I want you to come with me."

I was glad that my head was resting on his shoulder so he couldn't see the expression on my face. I rearranged my features so I didn't look so shocked, then pulled back to look him in the eye.

"I can't fly!"

He just grinned lazily back at me. "No, but I can." He gave me a wink and pulled me back to him. I wasn't sure if the thumping in my chest was from nerves about tomorrow or the thrill of the now.

Chapter Ten

barely slept a wink that night. Every time I closed my eyes I could feel myself soaring through the sky. As I finally drifted off to sleep, I woke with a jolt, free-falling through the sky only to find myself safe and warm in the bed.

The morning dawned in much the same way as the previous one, with all the dragons eating breakfast together around the huge campfire and the wonderful smell of food cooking. I gave Edeline a warm grin as I sat in the circle with the dragons. Lucy immediately came over to me and gave me a hug, and even the others smiled at me and said hello. As I looked around at the group of thirty or so people, it struck me once again just how close they all were. Every meal was like a party—festive, friendly and full of fun although the band was no longer there. I looked around for Ash and found him at the other side of the fire talking to two young men. He turned and saw me so I waved, thinking he'd wave back. Instead, he brought the two men over to meet me.

"Julianna, this is Stone and Ally. They're my hunting partners and the ones we'll be with today."

I looked up at the pair of them. Both were at least a head taller than Ash and you could tell right away that they were brothers, more than likely twins as they were so similar with chiseled jawlines and easy-going smiles. Curiously, one had hair so dark it was almost black and caramel-colored skin with eyes like chocolate. His brother was pale, with white-blond hair and eyes the color of the sky. It was as if they were negatives of each other

"Hello," I said shyly, holding out my hand to shake theirs. They both took my hand and kissed it in turn, causing me to blush and Ash to roll his eyes.

"They both think they are God's gift to women but don't be fooled by their charms. They're really a couple of idiots." Ash grinned as he said this and I could tell that he was ribbing them.

"At least we aren't ugly, right, Ally?" retorted Stone, playfully punching Ash on the arm.

"Yeah," replied Ally, joining in the humor. "I don't know what you see in him personally. I've seen prettier gorillas."

They sat on either side of me, dark-haired Stone to my right and Ally to my left. I was blushing so hard at both their words and their presence that I could probably have rivaled their dragon fire with the heat in my cheeks.

Thoughts of flying through the air with these three, hunting for gazelle or some other food, had my nerves in tatters.

"I don't know how good I'll be at hunting with you guys," I said, bringing the conversation round to the day ahead, hoping the topic would stop my cheeks from burning.

"Don't worry," said Ash, standing in front of me with a plate of meat and bread that Lucy had just passed him. "We're not going to send you out to hunt before we train you. That's why I've roped in the moron twins here in to help.

"Oy!" said Ally, throwing a chunk of bread at Ash, which he ducked expertly. The bread fell into the fire to become toast.

"Nice try!" said Ash, doing a comical jig on the spot. "Let's hope you throw better than that in training!" Just then, another chunk of bread soared through the air, hitting him in the center of his forehead.

"Bullseye!" Stone and Ally high-fived, causing me to giggle. Today was going to be much more fun than I had anticipated and the fears I'd harbored were beginning to melt away.

Once breakfast was over, I was taken to another stone circle I'd not seen before. This one was much larger than the one with the campfire and had a white wooden wall at one side about fifteen feet long and six feet high. The circle looked a little like the training ground by my house although blackened stones and ash showed that they also practiced here in their dragon forms.

"We're going to start with hand-to-hand combat," said Ash, showing me a flat rock to sit on. "I'll let Ally and Stone go first just so you can see how we train."

"Yeah, and the fact that you are way too much of a chicken to go up against either of us," said Stone with a grin.

"Just fight, will you?" replied Ash, rolling his eyes once again.

Watching the two fight was almost like being at a dance. The way they moved together was almost magical; it was obvious that they had been fighting like this since they were young. It was almost brutal in nature and yet, despite the magnificently wild and fierce way that they moved, neither really wanted to hurt the other.

"Show offs," muttered Ash beside me as Stone brought Ally toppling to the ground, straddling him to stop him from getting back up. As Stone's hands flew into the air to mark himself a winner, I couldn't help but clap, much to Ash's annoyance.

"I win. Do I get to fight the fair lady now?" asked Stone, pulling himself off of his brother and dusting himself down.

"I'll fight with Julianna. You guys can watch," said Ash irritably. I couldn't help but smile. I'd never had anyone be jealous over me before, but I could sense it in Ash now and it made me feel warm inside. Any fears of fighting were long gone as we took our positions in the center of the circle while Stone and Ally sat where we had on the edge. Instead, butterflies filled my stomach for a completely different reason. I'd watched how Stone and Ally had fought, the beautiful yet savage way in which their bodies had moved together, and now here I was about to do the same with Ash.

"Don't worry. I'm not going to hurt you."

He must have seen the trepidation in my face that had nothing to do with getting hurt. One of the brothers whistled to start the fight. I had been practicing for so long with a sword in my hand that I had no idea what to do without it. With no clue how to bring him down, I charged at him with none of the finesse I'd seen in Stone and Ally's fighting.

He ducked to the side, catching me on my arm as he did. With a maneuver so quick I barely saw it, he had me on my back in the charred dirt.

"Round one to Ash," I heard someone say as Ash grabbed my hand and pulled me back up.

"Don't just run at me. I'm bigger than you. Use that to your advantage," whispered Ash as we faced each other again. That was all right for him to say but my heart was beating so loudly in my chest at the thought of being so close to him that I could barely concentrate. I also couldn't see how being smaller would put me at any kind of advantage in combat.

"Before you run at me, find my weakness."

I looked into his eyes, barely a foot away from me, and a strange intensity glowed back at me. Electricity flowed between us and I could hear him breathing as heavily as I was even though our first round had lasted mere moments. Then, without thinking I bridged the gap between us and kissed him. It was the quickest of pecks on the lips but it did the trick. I seized the moment of surprise, hooked my leg around his, and pushed his chest.

He fell backward, landing flat on the ground to the brothers' hollering and clapping.

I couldn't help but grin at the look of shock on his face as he stared up at me from the dusty ground.

"You said to find your weakness," I said coyly, holding my hand out to him to help him up as he had done with me.

The smile that cracked his face was so wide that it finally sent the shivers down my spine and goosebumps up my arm which had been threatening for the last two minutes.

It was only when Stone and Ally wolf-whistled that I realized exactly what I had done and my cheeks began to burn.

"I think it's about time we showed you how we train as dragons," said Ash, still grinning. I couldn't help but match his grin even though I felt like a loon for doing so.

"Come on guys." He motioned with his hand and Stone and Ally stood. They all walked over to the wooden wall I'd seen before and disappeared behind it. I could see the foreheads of Stone and

Ally and just the top of Ash's hair over the top. I was just about to follow to see what they were doing when someone flung a pair of trousers over the top, quickly followed by a sweater.

It dawned on me that this was the place they undressed to change into dragons, so I instead returned to the flat rock that Stone and Ally had just vacated.

Seconds later there was a huge roar and a blast of flame as one dragon took off into the sky. Judging by the black leathery skin, it could only be Stone. He was outstanding, long and graceful in the sky with a shimmer of green on his scales when the sun hit them at just the right angle.

A pure white dragon followed and then finally the scarlet dragon I recognized as Ash. They flew in perfect formation, swooping and twirling in the sky, putting on an aerial show just for me, before flying back down to the circle and landing with effortless grace. I couldn't believe I'd spent the whole night worrying about flying. Just watching them in the sky made me long to be up there with them. The sense of freedom they must feel would be breath-taking.

This time, they didn't fight in twos, but in a kind of free for all, each man—or dragon—for himself. Ash reared up, extending his claws and savagely laying into Stone who was snarling back at him, giving as much as he got. If I didn't know that they were friends and this was only training, I'd have been terrified at the beautiful savagery of it. Ally rose a couple of feet from the ground and rained fire down around them, causing Stone and Ash to break apart and fly after him.

This time, there was no stunning formation flying; they were fighting. Fire filled the sky, bathing it in flashes of warm red and orange. Even though they were quite a way above me, I could still feel the heat of their breath as they blew fire at each other. One of the brothers caught Ash square on in a burst of flame. Fear coursed through me as I stood up, peering into the fiery sky. I had to use my hand to shield my eyes but I saw him fly through the fire as if it wasn't there. I couldn't keep my eyes from him and how elegantly he flew, shooting between the two brothers as they both directed another blast of fire at him, accidentally getting each other instead. My heart was in my mouth the whole time that they were in the air, fearing for their safety, and I was glad when they all landed unscathed.

As they disappeared around the other side of the wall to dress, I realized that they were just like me, like us on the other side of the mountain. They ate together, lived together and trained together in perfect harmony. This new world was so similar to my old one and yet the two were like oil and water and could never mix. The time when I would have to choose between the two was drawing closer and with each passing moment, it was getting more and more difficult to know which decision I was going to make. If Ash had his way, I wouldn't have to decide at all. Both sides would live in harmony, but it wasn't just up to Ash.

As he appeared, fully clothed and completely burnfree from the side of the wall, I ran to him, determination coursing through me.

"We need to make this work!" I said, causing a look of confusion to appear on Ash's face.

"Make what work?"

"This!" I said breathlessly, indicating first myself, then him. "Us. All of us. I want to help the dragons!"

"You're already doing just that by being here and letting them see you mean no harm."

"We have to tell my family the truth but I don't know how. I don't want to hurt them."

"I know you don't. Neither do I. Come on, let's go home."

I held his hand. Something had changed within me. Maybe it was the kiss or maybe it was watching him and his friends train, but when he said we were going home, I knew that that was what this place was beginning to feel like.

CHAPTER ELEVEN

omeone yelling woke me early from my slumber. I'd slept like a log compared to the previous night, and the fear-filled nightmares I'd experienced the night before had been replaced by much happier dreams. My heart was filled with wonder and even the commotion outside my window and the noisy awakening could not dampen my spirits.

I dragged myself out of bed as the noise got louder. The night before, I'd asked Edeline if I could borrow some clothes and she'd graciously lent me some of hers. I pulled on a green summer dress which was only slightly too large for me and opened the balcony doors to see what was happening. Looking down to the campfire, I could see many of the dragons I'd already met, some in human form and some in dragon form, plus a few I didn't recognize. They were definitely arguing but from this height, I couldn't hear what they were saying.

I picked Ash out in the crowd. He was talking to one of the dragon men I'd seen around but not spoken to. When I saw the look on Ash's face, I knew something bad was happening. The man he was with waved his arms animatedly and looked angry. Ash was trying unsuccessfully to placate him, but there was a sadness I'd not seen before on his face. Even at this distance, I could tell that he was upset.

I ran down the stairs calling for Edeline and Lucy, but the only one who answered was Firecracker who bounded up to me with a woof and a wagging tail.

I patted her on the head absentmindedly.

"Not now, girl. Do you know where your mistress is?"

Firecracker responded with another bark.

I patted her once again and left the house to find out what was going on, making sure she was safely shut inside. There were so many people that it was impossible to see what had happened, but I could see the man prodding Ash in the chest angrily by the side of the cliff. No one had noticed me; they were all consumed by whatever it was that had happened, so I took the opportunity to sidle along the edge of the cliff to better hear.

When I was almost upon them, the angry man turned and saw me.

"You!" he roared. His voice was so loud it was enough to make everyone else silent. "This is your fault!" He turned his attention away from Ash and walked toward me, his face set in an angry grimace.

I couldn't help but hold my breath as he approached with angry strides. I had no idea what I had done but whatever it was, I'd made this man extremely angry. I'd spent the whole evening in my bedroom alone so I couldn't for the life of me think what it might be.

"You shouldn't have come here," he shouted. His face was incandescent with rage, and he was pointing his finger at me. I took a step back, hitting the base of the cliff. With the rock wall behind me, I was trapped. The man was one of those that had hugged me just a day ago. What could I possibly have done to evoke such anger in him within the last twelve hours? He prodded me in the same way I'd just watched him do to Ash.

"Leave her alone, Bill. She had nothing to do with it and you know it." Ash came up behind him and grabbed his arm, swinging him away from me. Bill pulled his other arm back as if to strike Ash, but he was too quick. Ash ducked and then spun, kicking Bill down into the dusty ground in much the same way I had done to him yesterday.

"If you touch her again, you'll get worse than that," said Ash, his own anger evident.

Bill turned and spat at the ground. "Just get her away from me and out of my sight."

"What's happening?" I asked fearfully. Everyone was looking at us, some of them with the same anger Bill had displayed, others only looking upset. Lucy had tears in her eyes.

"I'll tell her," said Ash to the others. To me, he simply said, "Follow me."

He took me back to the training ground where I had kissed him just a day ago. It had been the most wonderful day and yet here we were the next morning, and I knew that Ash was going to tell me something I didn't want to hear.

"What is it?" I looked into his pained eyes and held my breath.

"Stone was killed last night."

My hand flew to my mouth in shock as I gasped at the news. I could barely take it in. He'd been so vibrant and full of life.

"What happened?"

"He decided to go out to the other side of the cliff. Julianna, he was killed by one of the men in your village. A slayer murdered him."

I could barely comprehend what he was telling me and yet he had no reason to lie. One of my friends had killed him. One of my family even. I didn't need to ask what had become of his body. It would be taken into the village like all the others. The ones that were killed on special days, the first kills, were always taken to the village green where their body would be displayed whilst the village partied around it. It had never occurred to me to find out what happened to the bodies after that. Nor had I ever asked what had happened to the bodies of the dragons killed on the non-special days. They were probably left to rot somewhere on the outskirts of the village. Stone was dead and I didn't even know where he would be buried. I had never felt so utterly dreadful in my whole life.

I felt eyes bore into me and as I turned, my eyes met Ally's as he stood by the campfire. The others had gone back to crying and arguing and hugging each other, all of them dealing with the news of Stone's death differently, but Ally just stood there. He didn't look angry, just sad and lost, like a man who had misplaced his shadow.

I'd only met him the day before but he looked diminished without his dark-skinned twin next to him.

There was nothing I could do to bring his brother back to him and nothing I could say that would make this right, but as I looked at him, I tried to convey how sorry I was and how much my heart was breaking for him.

Edeline appeared then, wrapping her arms around him, and his eye contact with me broke.

I turned back to Ash and it was as if the dam inside me cracked. Tears fell onto the parched ground. Everything I had learned within the last few days had not prepared me for this moment. Even though I knew that my people had killed hundreds of dragons over the years, Stone's death finally made it real. Ash's arms circled around me as I cried. My body was wracked with quiet, anguished sobs. There was nothing I could do to make this better. My head filled with memories of easy-going Stone, how cute and how funny he had been. I couldn't believe it was only yesterday we had all sat around this very stone ring and I'd watched him train with Ally and Ash.

"I'm sorry," I murmured almost inaudibly. My face was buried in his chest. His arms tightened around me, making me feel safe. A feeling I had no right to have.

"Don't apologize. You've done nothing wrong."

"But Stone—"

"Stone shouldn't have even been on that side of the mountain. He knew the risks and chose to ignore them. We only go over there when we need to. Most of the time it's only to keep a look out, and even then we try to keep as far away from the slayers as possible. He was a grown man, and the decision that cost him his life was ultimately his."

"You didn't stay far away from me as possible," I said, remembering just how close he'd flown to me the day I had first walked up the mountain.

"Yeah, but I thought you were cute. I just wanted a better look."

I gave a sad laugh, more for his benefit than mine. He was trying to cheer me up but it felt as though my heart had been replaced with a heavy stone.

"Listen," he said, pulling away from me so he could look into my eyes. I couldn't bear to look at him so instead, I gazed at the ground. He gently placed two fingers under my chin and lifted my face until I had no choice. My face was a mess of tears and snot but I was too upset to care. Ash had no malice in his eyes. Instead, they showed nothing but kindness. If anything, it made me feel worse.

"No one blames you for what happened to Stone."

"Bill does," I reminded him.

"Bill is just upset. He doesn't know what he's saying. He worked with Stone. They were pretty close. He doesn't really blame you."

"Well, he should!" I shouted, feeling wretched. The anger inside me was nothing to do with Ash and everything to do with how I felt about myself. Anger and guilt and grief swirled through me. "It was my people that killed him."

"You're right!" he countered, his voice matching my own. "Your people. Not you. You didn't stab him with your sword. It wasn't your fault."

What was I doing? Why was I shouting at the one person who was on my side? I fell into him once again, needing his warmth and protection, desperate to feel his arms around me. He stroked my hair, calming me.

"This has to stop!" I said. "No more blood can be shed over some ridiculous, ancient feud. We need to put an end to this."

"That's exactly what I've been saying all along," replied Ash. "Between us, we have the power to put an end to this."

He gently pulled back a stray strand of hair and kissed me lightly on the cheek. Yesterday the action would have delighted me, but today I took little pleasure in it. I felt like all the happiness had been sucked out of me, leaving me empty and afraid.

Then, some other emotion came over me. I don't know whether it was because of Ash holding me or something I had inside me all along, but I suddenly felt a strength I had never known I possessed.

With every bone in my body, I vowed to put an end to this. Soon enough I'd have to speak to the other dragons, but for right now, I had Ash.

I pulled away from his arms and instead held his hand. I turned slowly to the grief-stricken villagers. If they hated me for Stone's death, I wouldn't blame them, but sooner rather than later

I'd have to answer to them. To the man who lost a workmate. To the brother that lost his twin and to the village that lost a son and friend. I'd have to answer to them all. I gripped Ash's hand tightly and took a step back to the campfire. I knew I had to be strong and with Ash beside me giving me courage, I had everything I needed in order to do what had to be done.

CHAPTER TWELVE

f I was nervous five minutes ago, it was nothing compared to how I felt when I saw Spear standing by the campfire. There were also many more people than I had previously met. They, like Spear, must have come from the houses in the village. With Ash by my side, I tried to hide my fear as I entered the circle of dragons. He'd managed to get them into some semblance of order and now the stone circle was filled with people all looking his way. I took the opportunity to sit toward the back in the hope that no one would see me.

The sound of sobbing still surrounded me but the chaos from ten minutes ago had subsided.

"Right!" said Spear. "I think everyone is here so I shall begin. As you all know, a courageous young man died last night..."

"He was murdered by a slayer, you mean," shouted someone although I couldn't tell who. I pushed myself farther back on the rock in an attempt to hide.

A couple of people jeered at his words.

"He was one of our very best," continued Spear, ignoring the man who had heckled him. "He will be sorely missed by all of us, but especially by Eleanor, Tom, and Ally."

An older couple stood next to Ally, presumably the twins' parents. The woman was crying into her husband's shoulder. My heart went out to them.

"Do you want to say a few words about Stone?" asked Spear to the couple. The old man set his mouth into a grim line as he shook his head and held onto his inconsolable wife. Ally pushed into the circle, taking Spear's place.

"I want to talk about my brother. He was my twin and my best friend." His voice cracked with the pain of speaking. "Everyone thinks that twins have this unique connection and it's true. It does exist. When Stone scraped his knee, I felt the pain in my own knee. When I fell out of a tree at the age of eleven and broke my arm, he went home complaining of a sore arm way before he knew I'd hurt myself. We knew what the other was thinking. He was half of me."

He broke down into loud sobs but didn't give up speaking. I could see that he needed us all to understand just how special Stone was, but I had a feeling everyone already knew.

"I can still feel him! How can that be if he's dead? How could I still feel him so strongly within me?"

A young woman I didn't know came up to him and threw her arms around his neck and gave him a tight squeeze.

"I'm sorry, Ally. I was out there with him. I saw them kill him. He's definitely dead."

"But I can feel him," he pleaded to the young girl before descending into uncontrollable crying. She led him away from the circle so that Spear could take his place again.

He began to talk about how connected they all were to this land and how they could never leave, but something about what Ally had said resonated within me. Of course, he could have been in denial about his brother's death and the weird twin connection thing could mean nothing, but what if he was right? What if Stone was out there somewhere? The woman had said that she had seen him die, but if his soul was trapped within the slayer's sword, then maybe that was why Ally was so sure he could still feel his existence. Because he wasn't dead at all. His soul was just not inhabiting his body.

Once the thought entered my mind, I couldn't shake it. Was Ally still alive out there somewhere? I thought of my own sword that I'd left in the bedroom in the cliff house and how it was supposed to be filled with the soul of a dragon by now. My father's sword was said to be filled with the souls of a hundred dragons. Before I'd come here, it had been nothing more than an abstract thought that didn't really mean anything. Sure, I knew the souls strengthened the swords, but I'd thought that dragons' souls were worth very little, that they didn't mean anything. The thought of a hundred or more of them trapped within my father's sword was enough to bring bile up my throat. It was worse than death, the thought of being trapped forever within a metal object.

I looked across to Ash who was listening intently to Spear speak. He was still talking about the connection they felt to the land and to each other, and how they could never leave, despite the danger on the other side of the cliffs. It became clear to me just why they felt so connected. The souls of their ancestors, their fathers and their brothers, were still here, albeit trapped at the other side of the cliff and they didn't even know it. The way Spear was talking about it being a spiritual connection was right. I had to tell someone! If it would bring Stone back, I'd stand in front of the whole crowd and speak myself.

I opened my mouth to tell Ash when I suddenly realized what telling them would mean. It wasn't as simple as getting the dragon souls back. They'd have to go to my village and take them back. By force.

Most of the villagers were trained dragon slayers. They'd fight to the death before even knowing who the dragons really were. Causalities would be high on both sides and then maybe it would be Jasper or my father that would get killed. Maybe it would be Ash.

"Come on," I heard Ash say, breaking me away from my thoughts. The people were beginning to disperse. It seemed the meeting was over. "We need to get you out of here."

I followed him silently as we ran behind the people into the cave house and shut the door. Firecracker came bounding over, her tail wagging enthusiastically.

"At least someone likes me," I said, giving her hair a friendly tousle.

"I like you," said Ash, coming toward me. He gazed at me with such concern in his eyes but something else too. It wasn't happiness. It was warmth and safety and friendship and something else I couldn't quite decipher. I couldn't look at him without the tears welling up. I couldn't help it. My eyes stung and I knew that if I held his gaze just one moment longer I was going to cry. He pulled me into a hug and the dam finally burst. I sobbed onto his shoulder, wetting his outfit. The hug could have lasted two minutes or two hours, I couldn't tell, but it was interrupted when Edeline and Lucy walked through the door.

"We'd be better stay indoors today," remarked Edeline. "I think a storm might be brewing. We'll eat away from the others in here."

I glanced out the window. There wasn't a cloud in the sky. The storm she was talking about had nothing to do with the weather.

The day passed slowly. I hung out with Ash up in my bedroom, and we sunbathed a little on the terrace. He tried to engage me in conversation but I was so distracted with thoughts of the slayers' swords that I wasn't much of a conversationalist. We ate dinner there until great black clouds blew in. Maybe Edeline was right after all. When the first big, fat, heavy drops of rain began to fall from the sky, we moved indoors.

"Are you okay?" he asked as he closed the door to the outside. "You've been quiet all day."

"I'm sorry. Today has been hard. I just need some space." His face fell as I said the words but it was true. I knew he was hurting too, and I had the feeling that he'd been glued to my side all day because he needed company, but my company wasn't worth much at the moment. He'd been wonderful to me but the truth was I felt guilty about getting him into this. He shouldn't be inside with me; he should be outside with his friends so they could all share their grief. "Goodnight then," he said, kissing my cheek sadly.

I watched him go, leaving me alone with only my own misery for company. It was early but I flopped onto the bed, listening to the hammering of the rain against the window. Usually, I loved the sound.

I tried sleeping but the thought of those dragons locked within the swords was haunting me. Guilt had me lying awake for so long that it was completely dark before I eventually got to sleep. I couldn't have been asleep long before a huge roll of thunder rattled the windows. I sat up in bed, fearful of the noise, before I realized what it was that had woken me.

Someone needed to find out if we could get the souls back from the swords. I jumped out of bed and put on the warmest clothes I could find. I also attached my armor and sword, not because I thought I would have to fight anyone, but because I wasn't sure if I'd make it back.

I crept quietly through the house, only disturbing Firecracker who was her usual exuberant self. Thankfully, she didn't bark as I let myself out into the night. The rain was pounding down, making it difficult to see, but I only had to follow the cliff to get to where I'd seen the stairs cut out of it earlier. I had no idea if they would lead me up over them, but I had to try. I couldn't bring myself to look at the circle where we had trained only a day or so ago. It only reminded me of Stone.

By the time I came upon the steps, my clothes were soaked and I was freezing cold. It was too late to turn back though. Someone had to save those dragons and that someone had to be me. I placed my foot on the first step and looked up. The steps seemed to go on forever. It was going to be a long and arduous journey but in my heart, I knew it was one I had to make. I whispered a goodbye to Ash and started the journey up the cliff face.

CHAPTER CHIRTEEN

he rain lashed down as I fought my way up the mountainside. The going was tough as each step was slippery and the wind blew a gale in my face. I clung to the rocks, drenched to the bone and fearful for my life. The steps were narrow and, without a rail of any kind, it would be easy to take a misstep and fall to my death. I could barely see a thing with the rain stinging my eyes and the darkness of the clouds. There would be no moonlight or starlight to help me out tonight. Using my sense of touch, I climbed the dangerous path, feeling my way along the wet roughness of the rocky cliff face. My eyes were stinging so much that I couldn't tell if it was from the rain or tears. Nothing rivaled the pain in my chest though. Not my stinging eyes or my body that screamed with the blistering cold of the storm. My armor weighed heavy as I trudged upward, each step feeling like a mountain all on its own.

I tried to think of something, anything, to keep my mind from the agony in my hands and feet as the cold bit down hard. I thought of Ash, asleep in his bed, and the pain became unbearably worse because now it was inside my heart as well. The thought that he would wake up the next day and I'd be gone filled me with such guilt, but what choice did I have? It was the only way to get Stone and the others back. I could almost see the moment when he would wake up and realize I'd gone home. He'd think I was betraying him, wouldn't he? And yet I felt that he knew me. When he looked into my eyes, it felt like he saw into my very soul. He had to know that I wouldn't leave if it wasn't important.

I couldn't get the image of him out of my mind all the way up the cliff face, and when I reached a platform with a cave, I'd have done anything to have him by my side. The cave mouth was a wide, gaping chasm and without any light flooding it

from outside, I couldn't see more than a foot or two
into it. I should have turned back but when I saw
how far I'd come, the thought left me. It was the
image of Stone and the reason I was doing this in
the first place that spurred me on. I had made my
way up the cliff face in almost complete blackness
just by feeling the wall. If I could make it this far, I
could keep going.

My hands waved in front of me as I felt my way
into the inky blackness. Just a couple of feet in, I
stumbled on something and tumbled to the ground,
banging my knees and making my armor clatter as
it hit the hard floor of the cave. I reached out,
hoping to find something that would help pull me
up into an upright position, but when I scrabbled
around I felt something much better—a long stick
with a cloth around the end. If there was a torch
here, there must be some way to light it.

I was proficient in making fires—it was all part
of the slayer training—but I needed some flint to
make a spark. I'd also not tried setting fire to cloth,
always using dry twigs and paper, but I could smell
the bitter odor of some kind of fire accelerant

emanating from the cloth so I knew it would light pretty quickly. I felt around the floor near where I'd found the torch until my hand came upon a smooth flint stone. Luckily, the floor inside the cave was dry so I ripped the flint along the floor just near the head of the torch. Sparks flew, lighting up the cave for a fraction of a second before it was once again plunged into darkness. I tried it again, this time getting as close to the torch as possible.

A spark hit the torch, igniting the accelerant and bathing the cave in a warm orange glow. Relief flooded through me that I could finally see. This cave, like the other one, went back much further than just a few feet. Even with the light of the torch, I couldn't see the back. I walked forward, keeping my eyes on the ground for any more loose stones. If I were to fall and injure myself, I might end up stuck up here forever.

I followed the tunnel deep into the cave. My spirits were beginning to rise, knowing that it wouldn't take too long to get through the mountain as long as I kept in a straight line. This, however, was where my luck ran out. I came to a T-junction with my only options being left or right, neither of which were the direction I wanted to go. I waved the torch down each corridor, but both were equally uninteresting and neither looked like a way out. I took the path on the right just because it bent slightly to the left. After another ten minutes of walking, the path forked again. I scoured the floor and walls, looking for some kind of sign that someone might have left, but found nothing.

"What did you think you'd find? A glowing sign reading this way out?" I asked myself. The sound echoed hauntingly around the walls, doing nothing to calm my frayed nerves.

I'd heard about a trick to use when stuck in a maze, for this was a maze and if I ventured deeper, I'd surely lose my way. It was something about picking a direction, left or right, and sticking to it until I found my way out, but that didn't seem right. If I took another right turn, I'd end up heading back towards the cliff face and that was the complete opposite of where I needed to be. I took the left-hand tunnel, hoping for the best, even though I had lost my sense of direction.

I had never felt so alone in my life as I did in that tunnel, trapped between two different worlds. The darkness scared me more than I liked to admit. Even though the torch light covered everything within a few feet, I saw nothing at all beyond its reach. The lullaby my mother sang to me on the morning of my eighteenth birthday popped into my head. It kept my heart warm, thinking of it as I walked through the network of paths, my decisions based on intuition instead of reasoning. I must have been walking at least half an hour before deciding I was hopelessly and terrifyingly lost.

Suddenly, there was a huge whoosh and the torch went out, plunging me into darkness. Then the wind came again followed by an intense heat as flames licked the ceiling of the cave. I screamed, wondering what could cause such a strange phenomenon until a large dragon with a pair jeans in one claw came around the corner. I only caught a glimpse before the fire stopped, but it was enough. I'd recognize those red scales anywhere. It was Ash. He'd come to rescue me.

I held the torch aloft, waiting for him to breathe fire again. When he did, I held out the torch and watched it ignite before turning away from him to give him the chance to turn back.

"Why are you leaving?" he asked a few moments later. I turned to find him fastening the top button of his jeans. He wasn't angry. It was fear in his eyes. Putting the torch down carefully, I ran to him and threw my arms around his neck. He felt so warm and yet the hug was awkward thanks to all the armor. I couldn't help but begin to sob again as he held onto me, comforting me, making me feel dreadful because it should have been me comforting him.

"I'm sorry," I finally said as I pulled back. "I have to go home."

"Without telling me?" I could see the pain in his eyes matching my own.

"I couldn't tell you because I didn't want to hurt you or get your hopes up, but I think there might be a way to get Stone back. That's why I left."

"He's dead, Julianna. You heard it yourself. One of your people killed him."

I blanched at his words but I had to make him believe me.

"We don't kill just because of centuries of hatred. Each kill we make is said to take the soul of a dragon that imbues our swords with power. It's their soul that the sword takes, not their life. I've not once seen where the dragon's bodies are taken after death. What if they are all lying somewhere in an eternal slumber? Alive and yet empty at the same time?"

He regarded me for a second as I willed him to believe me.

"You don't kill the dragons?"

"I don't know, but what if I'm right? I have to try to find out. I was planning to go to my village and see if I could somehow get the souls out of the swords."

"I just don't understand why you didn't tell me all of this before. I'd have come with you. I want to protect you."

"I know." His words made me feel guilty and yet elated at the same time. He had protected me throughout all of this and yet hearing him say it filled my heart. "I didn't want to put you in danger. I'm scared that the other dragons will turn against you because of me."

He came closer and held me tightly once again. This time, I managed to keep the tears at bay.

"I'm a big boy, Julianna. I know how to handle myself. I don't want you to worry about me, but there is something you can do for me."

"What is it?" I asked, pulling back slightly so I could see him.

"I want you to tell me everything from now on. We're in this together and the only way we can do this is if we are honest with each other."

"I'll never lie to you again. I promise."

"Good." He took hold of my hand. "Now let's go to your village and find these swords."

He held my hand, expertly guiding me through the maze until we were at the other side. In the distance, the lights of my village seemed small and insignificant, especially from this great height.

Minutes later I was soaring through the rain on Ash's red-scaled back. I was finally going home.

CHAPTER FOURTEEN

ater stung my eyes as we flew through the angry clouds, blinding me for the whole journey. I trusted Ash to know what he was doing and only hoped that his dragon vision was better than my human eyesight as we flew down the mountains.

The rain came down in hundreds and thousands of big, fat drops that not only drenched me, but Ash's clothes that were squeezed in my hands. Only I would be crazy enough to pick the wettest night of the summer to sneak out.

We landed just outside of the village with a great thump. Lightning crackled across the sky, illuminating the small houses for the briefest of moments. The darkness of the night and the clouds kept us in the shadows and made me feel grateful for the storm, even though I was soaked through and freezing cold. I threw Ash his clothes and walked to the fence that marked the border between the village and the mountains. All the houses were dark. However, in the distance, I could make out the road that would take us to my house. I turned and gazed up at the mountain we had flown down from, holding my hand above my eyes to shield them from the pelting rain that still came down in torrents. The mountain range was shrouded in clouds to the tree line, almost like the towering peaks weren't there at all.

"What now?" asked Ash, making me jump. He'd changed and dressed already, the sound of the rain hitting the pathway beneath us covering the sound of him changing.

"I need to go home."

"Do you think that's a good idea?" he asked. Concern filled his voice and I understood why. He thought that I wanted to see my parents. In a way, he was right. I missed them terribly, maybe even Jasper too, but that wasn't the only reason.

"It's the only place I know where some of the swords are kept. My brother, Jasper, has one, and my father too. His is said to be one of the most powerful swords in the village."

"Does that mean he's taken the most dragon souls?"

I nodded, unable to speak. I'd spent my whole life looking up to my father, wanting to follow in his footsteps. I could barely believe that I was now planning to break into my own house and steal his sword. What would he think of me if we got caught? I wasn't even sure what I thought of him anymore. "I'm sorry."

He kissed the top of my forehead. "You have nothing to be sorry about."

I heard his words, but, not for the first time, I wasn't sure if they were true.

The road to our house was deserted and yet we kept to the trees, partly for the cover they offered from the rain, but mainly because if anyone were to turn their lights on, we could dash into their cover.

The rain had turned the usually dusty track into a muddy bog. Ash held my hand as we trekked through it, giving me the strength to do what I had to do and reminding me how important it was that we did this.

"Do you think you'll know?" I whispered, as we approached my house.

"Know what?"

"Will you know whose soul is in each sword when we get close to one? Will you be able to feel it?"

"I don't know. I don't feel anything other than freezing at the moment. Are we nearly there?"

"This is it. This is where I live."

The house looked almost deserted with the lack of light but I knew it was because it was late enough for them all to be asleep.

There was no way to hide as we snuck across the training ground in front. It was a wide-open space with the house on the opposite side. We could only hope that the darkness and the lateness of the hour would be enough to get us to the house without being seen.

The back door was locked but my mother always kept a spare key under a potted plant near the door in case of emergencies. I picked the pot up and scrabbled around in the muddy earth beneath it.

"It's not there!" I whispered.

"What isn't?" asked Ash, falling to his knees to help me look.

"The spare key. My mother always has one under this pot and it's gone. Can you see it?"

"No. There's nothing there but mud."

"Why wouldn't it be here?" I asked, wiping my muddy hands on my tunic.

"You've been gone for a few days now. Maybe they think we'll come for them next."

"That's ridiculous," I replied.

"They lost a daughter. They're scared. People do strange things when they're scared. Is there another way in?"

The thought of my father being scared of anything was preposterous. He was the bravest man I had ever known. And yet...he never lost a daughter before.

167

"I think there might be a crowbar in the shed," I replied, trying not to feel overcome with emotion. We had a plan and we needed to stick to it.

I left Ash by the back door and ran to the shed. We never locked it as there were only a few tools that weren't worth a lot, but as Ash had said, things had changed. I closed my eyes and said a silent prayer before pulling on the door handle. It opened immediately; however, in the darkness, I couldn't see the crowbar. We kept all kinds of junk in here as well as tools—too-small bikes from our childhoods, bits of broken furniture that my father hadn't gotten around to fixing, and the miscellany that families accumulate over time. I could spend all day going through it all and not find the crowbar, especially in the dark.

I ran back to Ash and told him the problem.

"Use your sword," he suggested. "Slot it in the crack between the door and the frame and jimmy the door open."

I pulled my sword from its sheath and did as he instructed. After a few pushes the wooden door splintered with a crack and opened.

Thankfully, at the same moment, a roll of thunder crashed, hiding most of the noise.

"Are you okay?" whispered Ash.

"I just feel weird having to sneak into my own house," I replied. I looked around the kitchen, remembering the last time I'd been in here. The morning of my eighteenth birthday, we'd had a huge breakfast to get us ready for my first day of slayer training.

I thought about stealing a sword and it occurred to me that perhaps my father's wouldn't be the best one to go for after all. "I think we'll go for Jasper's sword."

"I thought your father's sword held the most dragon souls. Surely it makes sense to go for his so we can release more of my people."

"We need to check if my theory is correct first. We can do that with either of the swords, but Jasper's will be easier to get. He keeps it propped up against the wall in his room. My father's is in a locked cabinet in my parent's bedroom. We'll never be able to get it without waking either of my parents up."

He was eager to know if I was right about the whole thing, and excited to free his friends, family and ancestors, but if we got caught, my father would make sure that neither of us would have the opportunity to be near a sword again.

I held my forefinger to my lips to indicate we should be quiet. The noise of the rain was much less intense inside although I could still hear it tapping on the windows. Ash stayed behind me the whole way up the stairs until we reached the landing. How easy it would be to go through my own door and fall into a nice warm bed and forget the last week had ever happened. But it had happened and as long as I lived, I didn't think I'd ever forget it.

My father's snoring rattled the windows from the inside almost as much as the rain did. I pulled down the handle on the door to Jasper's room and pushed silently. The room was almost pitch black, making everything difficult to see, but I could hear his much quieter snoring coming from the general direction of his bed.

I tiptoed in and gazed around the room, trying to make out the shape of the sword in the shadows, but it was too dark. I couldn't see much at all.

"I've got it," a voice whispered quietly into my ear. Ash had found the sword straight away. How had he done it? Had he sensed his ancestors nearby or had it merely been that his eyesight was a lot better than mine in the dark?

He passed me the sword which I had to hold in my hand as my own sword was filling up my sheath.

"Let's go!" I turned to follow him out the door, but in my haste to leave, I knocked over something that made a loud crash on the floor by my feet.

Suddenly, light flooded the room, making me blink in surprise.

I should have run but the shock at finding my brother sitting up in bed, his eyes on the sword in my hands, was enough to have me rooted to the spot.

"Julianna?" he asked, the shock at finding me in his room evident on his face. "What are you doing?"

CHAPTER FIFTEEN

For a split second, he didn't notice Ash, but as his eyes widened, focusing on something behind my right shoulder, I knew he had been seen and that our chance to run had passed.

"What's this?" growled Jasper, jumping out of bed. I stepped back as he bounded towards me.

"Jasper, I can explain—" I began but he cut me off before giving me the chance to say anything else.

"Explain? Are you going to tell me why you're in my bedroom with whoever this is, trying to steal my sword?"

"This is Ash, he's..." How could I explain who Ash was? If I told Jasper he was a dragon, Jasper

173

would go for him without listening to anything else I had to say. Jasper always had a tendency to react first, think later. We needed to get out of here.

I turned to tell Ash to run, but as I did, the sword was pulled from my hand. Jasper had taken the weapon back and now stood ready to fight, his sword arm raised.

"Jasper, don't!" I whispered. "This isn't what you think it is."

"So you aren't stealing my sword? Because that's what this looks like to me."

My hesitation was all he needed. The sword came swiping down at me and I only missed getting hit because Ash pulled me backwards quickly.

"I thought so," said Jasper, getting back into his stance and looking from Ash to me.

"I don't want to fight you, Jasper. You remember what happened last time we fought. I beat you."

"Yes, well this time is different," he growled. I guess he still hadn't forgiven me for beating his behind the last time we fought. He must be angry to strike before I even had a chance to draw my sword.

He was right though. This time was different. This time, we weren't training. This time, it was real. Someone was going to get hurt. I unsheathed my sword and copied his stance, hoping that when he saw how real the situation was, he'd back down, but he didn't. My decision to fight only angered him further. He thrust his sword forward, aiming for my stomach. I jumped back, just avoiding it by millimeters. Had he managed a hit there, it would have killed me. What was he doing?

"Jasper, stop!" It was my last-ditch attempt to not have to fight him. My back was now literally against the wall. If he tried anything else, I would have to defend myself and I wasn't experienced enough to fight him without hurting him.

He answered by swinging his sword again. I had no choice but to bring my own sword down against it to deflect it. He recovered quickly and tried again, but I was ready for him. I thrust my own sword forward, trying to nick his hand so he would drop the sword.

Out of the corner of my eye, I could see Ash, his wide eyes bouncing around the room, searching for a way out of the fight I was now embroiled in. But there was no way out. At least not with me in tow. If I ran now, Jasper would only follow and would be much quicker with his dry pajamas than I would be with my rain-soaked clothes and armor. Of course, the armor offered some protection against injury, but it wasn't the best, and he knew which bits of me were unprotected.

We both skirted the room, occasionally thrusting and deflecting. I was at the advantage with my armor, but only one of us was fighting to hurt and that wasn't me. I had no need to win except to finish the fight and get away, but if I only spent my time deflecting his sword, we'd be here all night. It wasn't helping that my wet clothes felt like ten-ton weights, severely impeding my reaction time and movements.

The only way to end this was to get the sword or to injure him. I didn't know how to do the first without having to resort to the latter.

Something in the air changed and it took me a few moments to realize what it was. The room was suddenly much quieter. Had the rain stopped pounding the windows? No, I could still hear it lashing down. It was then that I realized what it was. My father's snoring had stopped. Either he'd turned over in bed or the commotion had woken him up.

The door to my father's bedroom opened and I heard his footsteps on the landing.

Jasper must have heard it too. He hesitated for a moment, and that's when I struck. I hit the handle of his sword hard enough to make him drop it. The sword clanged to the floor just as my father came into the room.

"Julianna?"

I stood there with my sword outstretched, pointing the blade at Jasper who had his hands raised as though I were about to hurt him. Ash was on my right, closest to my father. From my father's point of view, it must have looked pretty bad.

"Who are you? What did you do to my daughter?" he bellowed, lunging toward Ash who dodged to the side quickly.

"Daddy!" I screamed as he knocked over a bookcase, sending books scattering all over the floor. "Stop it!"

"What did he do to you?" he asked me, running after Ash again who cut between Jasper and me to escape him.

"Annie, fetch my sword!" my father shouted to my mother who must have still been in their bedroom.

I wanted to hold up my sword to my father to stop him chasing Ash. He was so much bigger than him and I knew if he caught him, Ash wouldn't survive to tell the tale. And yet, I couldn't do that to my own father. What if he got hurt? Besides, if I took my sword away from Jasper for a second, he'd be able to retrieve his own from where it lay on the floor.

My father passed me, nearly tripping over Jasper's sword. When he saw it, he bent down himself to pick it up.

"I've got you now!" shouted my father to Ash, who had run back to the open doorway. He lifted Jasper's sword and charged at the defenseless Ash. Without thinking, I jumped in front of the sword to stop. My intention had been to jump into it right where my armor was, but I missed slightly and the sword sliced a thin red line into the flesh of my forearm. It wasn't a deep cut—it wouldn't even need stitches—but the shock at what he had done was enough to stop my father from trying again.

A scream from just outside the bedroom door had us all silent. I looked to my left to see my mother holding my father's sword. She looked so tiny with it in her hands.

"It's okay; it's just a scratch," I said, trying to appease her although she could just as well have been screaming at the sight of Ash in the doorway. The whole thing was a great big mess, and I didn't know how to deal with it. For now, everyone stood still with shock, paralyzed by the fear of what would happen next. If my father got his own sword, Ash would not get away again. My father was the most skilled swordsperson in the whole village.

One of us had to move soon and I knew it should be me, but I couldn't budge.

"Julianna, you're home!" My mother ran forward to hug me, dropping my father's sword in the process. From then on, it was as if everything happened in slow motion. I moved toward my mother to embrace her while my father and Jasper both ran for the falling sword. Ash grabbed my arm and started to pull me to the door.

While all this was going on, something infinitely stranger was happening. Jasper's sword began to emit smoke from the tip. The hissing made us all turn our heads to look at it. Because of it, my father's sword hit the floor before either my father or Jasper could catch it, my mother and I didn't get to hug each other, and Ash completely forgot about our escape. The lurid purple smoke had us all mesmerized as it blossomed into a thick fog. There was a loud bang from the sword itself, followed by a bright orange flame that lit up the room in a flash before going out completely, but not before setting fire to Jasper's curtains.

Ash grabbed my hand and pulled me down the stairs and out into the wet night. I could barely keep up with him as my feet sunk into the thick mud. My clothes were now so heavy with rain that each footstep caused me pain and the armor rubbed against my bare arms, making them chafe.

Behind us, my father was hot on our heels with Jasper and my mother following behind. I screamed, not because of my family chasing me, but because of what I could see behind them. Flames licked the side of our house in the distance, illuminating the dark sky and turning it a deep orange.

"Ash, do something!" I yelled. Villagers opened their doors and windows to see what the commotion was all about, and yet Ash pulled me onwards.

"I can't do anything. I can only make fire. I can't put it out. The rain will do that if it keeps up like this."

He hopped over the fence and into the woods at the base of the mountains and I followed, knowing it was our only chance of escape. If he couldn't save

181

my house, there was no reason for us to stick around. I turned and looked at my parents and brother one last time before disappearing into the trees. At least I knew they were all safe from harm. Before me, Ash's shape changed. He'd turned so quickly that his clothes ripped to shreds. I jumped onto his back and held onto his neck as he outstretched his wings, flying through a gap in the branches. It was only when we were half way up the mountain that I realized we had failed to steal either sword.

CHAPTER SIXTEEN

Befefore us, dark clouds covered the sky with a blanket of black, but behind us, fire painted the landscape every shade of orange.

"It's spreading!" I shouted pointlessly as the roar of the rain took my words away.

I could barely see my village anymore but the reach of the fire was unmistakable. The rain wasn't even touching it.

"Turn around!" I screamed out in a panic but Ash either didn't hear me or chose to ignore me.

We flew deeper into the clouds and the orange faded into black until there was nothing at all, and I once again had to close my eyes to block out the rain.

When we landed back on the ledge where I had first met Ash as a human, I immediately jumped from his back and ran to the edge. Freezing needles of rain lashed down, stinging my face, and yet I couldn't bring myself to enter the cave system which I knew would shelter me. Ash grabbed my arm and dragged me backwards until the darkness of the cave swallowed me.

"Why didn't you go back?" I shouted at him. "We shouldn't have left. All we succeeded in doing is burning my house and goodness knows how many others in my village to the ground. We didn't even bring a sword back except for mine and that's no use." I shook as I shouted, whether with fear, anger or cold, I didn't know, though it was probably a combination of all three.

"The rain will put it out. I already told you that. You need to get out of those clothes before you freeze to death. Your lips are practically blue with the cold."

"You didn't see how bad it was. It only looked like a small fire when we took off, but from a distance, it lit up the whole sky."

"Even a small fire would do that. You saw your family escape and your house was far enough away to not pose a danger to the other houses in the village. If it were a dry, hot day, maybe a stray ember might drift over and catch a straw roof, but look at the rain. The fire will be out in no time."

He moved towards me to hug me and for the first time since meeting him, I backed away from his embrace. It might have been irrational, but I was angry at him.

"Why didn't you turn around when I asked you? Even if you didn't think it was anything to worry about, you should have still listened to me."

"Julianna, if you want to go back, I'll take you back now. They're your family, and if you want to be there, we can go down the mountain. I didn't turn around because I didn't hear you."

"You mean it?"

"Of course! I don't know how you'll be able to help them but I wouldn't keep you away from them.

185

Look, the rain is starting to let up. Get out of those clothes before you get pneumonia and I'll dry them with my dragon breath. There's a blanket behind that rock; wrap yourself in it and when the rain stops, I'll take you home."

I ran towards him and gave him the hug I'd dodged earlier. It was only then I noticed he was dressed.

"You have clothes on! They were ripped to shreds back in the village."

"I keep a few spares up here. At least, I used to. I'm going through them so quickly I'll have to bring more up. This is my last set."

I picked up the blanket with the intention of getting undressed behind it, but Ash disappeared into the tunnel to let me change in private. He was right; I was freezing and could barely keep my teeth from chattering.

I put my armor to one side and peeled the sodden clothes from my body, laying them out as straight as I could on some rocks. The blanket was dry but not warm enough to make my goosebumps disappear or keep my teeth from chattering.

A wall of flame shot up the tunnel, quickly followed by Ash. He curled his body in the small cave and blew breathed more fire. The cave turned a bright orange and heated immediately. I could see he was being careful not to burn me or my clothes. The heat flowing through the small cave and the intermittent light made the cave feel homely. I'd spent time with Ash as a dragon before, but in all of those times, I'd been flying on his back. To have him sitting near me like this felt weird. I could talk to him but he wouldn't be able to answer me.

"Thank you for agreeing to take me home," I said to him.

It was hard to tell but I thought he nodded his head slightly. I could barely see him at all when he wasn't breathing fire, and when he did, his whole body reflected the light of the flames as though he was on fire himself.

I pulled the blanket tighter, thinking of my parents. Ash was right about one thing. They and Jasper had gotten out of the house without injury. I loved my house, but at the end of the day, that's all it was—a building full of things. The things that made it a home had all escaped the fire.

"I wonder what started the fire?" I asked out loud, not expecting an answer. I thought back to the scene in the bedroom before the curtains caught fire. There hadn't been a naked flame nearby. "I don't suppose you can produce fire in your human form can you?"

Ash made a growling noise which could have meant anything but he accompanied it by shaking his head. He blew another blast of heat my way, warming me right to my toes.

It had looked like the flame had erupted from Jasper's sword but how could it? It was made of metal and no part of it was flammable. I picked up my own sword and examined it. It was different from Jasper's but not so much to make any difference to its capability to catch fire. I admired the intricate metal work. When Ash blew another blast, I held up my sword in the path of the flame. The heat slightly burnished the metal but set no part of it alight.

I knew nothing about the slayer's swords. Not only could I not see how it could produce or sustain fire, I also couldn't see how it would trap a soul. Why had I not been taught any of this? I'd spent my whole life being taught swordlore and yet I knew nothing at all.

My thoughts went back to Stone and all the other dragons who had lost their souls at the hands of the people in my village. Going home now would serve no purpose other than to alleviate my fears. What would my parents do if I went home anyway? Jasper had been so angry to see me with Ash that he'd attacked me without even thinking to ask why I was home. My father wasn't any better. He'd jumped to the conclusion that Ash had kidnapped me, and like Jasper, he had attacked without pausing to find out who he was. That was the problem with the people in my village. They mindlessly followed hundreds of years of traditions without pausing to question why they were doing what they were doing.

"I'm not going home." I'd made a promise to Ash and I was going to keep it. I moved to sit beside him, snuggling as close as I could to his curled body and resting my arm on his skin. For so many years I'd believed dragon hide to be tough and scaly and cold, but Ash's skin was warm and comfortable. He brought his long neck around so I was completely surrounded. I rested my head on his neck and closed my eyes, listening to the rhythm of the rain on the ledge outside the cave.

Later when I awoke, the sun was beaming down, warming the cave. I stepped away from Ash, who was still sleeping in his dragon form, and grabbed my now dry clothes. Throwing them on, I stepped outside into the most radiant sunshine. Any evidence of the summer storm that had made me feel so cold the night before had gone, evaporated in the sunny morning. It was almost as if I'd dreamed the whole thing.

I peered down the mountain, trying to see my village, but of course, we were too far away. Now that the adrenaline had stopped pumping through me quite so freely and I'd had a decent amount of sleep, I knew I'd made the right decision to stay. Ash could try and convince the dragons to give the slayers a chance, but unless he had one on his side, his endeavors would be pointless. Despite what my parents and Jasper saw last night, or thought they saw, they knew me well enough to know how much I loved them, and the time would come when I'd be able to get the chance to put things right with them. Until then, there were plenty of families in the village that would take them in and make sure they were all right. Knowing the villagers as I did, they had probably already started rebuilding our house.

A warm pair of arms wrapped themselves around me. "You just say the word and I'll fly you back down there. I'll never stop you from going home."

"I know, and that's exactly the reason I need to stay." I brought my arms up to his and we just stood there like that for a long time, looking out at the incredible view down the mountain, the heat of the sun beating down on our faces.

We followed the same path through the mountain that we had taken the very first day I'd met Ash. This time, I had no problem holding his hand as we walked through the dark tunnel. Had

191

that really been less than a week ago? It felt so strange that I'd gone eighteen years with everything being the same and nothing really changing, and then in just a few days, my whole life had turned upside down; now everything was different.

We came out onto the ledge at the opposite side of the mountain and it became apparent very quickly that something was happening. There were dragons everywhere. Previously, I'd only ever seen two or three in the sky at once, but now it seemed the whole sky was full of them. They looked amazing, so many different shapes and sizes, a kaleidoscope of colors circling around.

"Uh oh!"

"What?" I asked Ash. "What's happening?"

"They're looking for us. They've probably been on the other side of the mountain too. We need to get you home quickly."

He pulled his shirt off without even bothering to run back into the cave to change.

"Wait!" I yelled as he began to undo the buttons on his trousers. "I already told you. I don't want to go home. I want to stay here with you."

"I meant my home!" he said, flinging his trousers off and changing into a dragon before my eyes. I scooped his clothes up and jumped onto his back as dragons swooped towards us. Unlike the leisurely flight I'd first taken down this mountain, this one was fraught with panic. The other dragons weren't attacking us, but as soon as they had caught sight of us, they had formed a formation around us to escort us back down to the ground.

CHAPTER SEVENTEEN

ind whipped my face as we soared past the training grounds toward the center of the village. The thatched roof of the circular Town Hall greeted me. We flew over a village square that had been hidden before.

The square was surrounded by shops made in the same higgledy-piggledy construction as the rest of the buildings in the village. Many had flat roofs with stairs leading to the ground. Some of the dragons descended onto these makeshift landing pads, although most of them, like us, landed in the square itself. To one side of the square was a cafe with tables and chairs arranged outside. On any other day, in any other situation, I'd have liked to sit there and drink a hot mug of coffee while watching the world go by.

The ground was still damp from the previous night's rain and large puddles had formed, leaving less space for the dragons to land. When they did land, they immediately ran to the edge of the square where two fences had been erected. They were the same type of dressing rooms I'd seen at the training ground just the other day.

I hopped off in the middle of the square and Ash flew to one of the fences to join his fellow dragons.

I'd not had time to count just how many dragons had escorted us back, but there were a lot. Many more in their human forms had been in the village square, waiting for us to return. The way they watched me made me extremely nervous. The noise of the bones crunching as the dragons changed still made me feel queasy, but it was the fear of what would happen next that made my stomach churn the most. I was alone and exposed, but there was nothing I could do but wait. I crossed my fingers, hoping that Ash would be the first to change, but it was Spear that made his appearance first. I almost didn't recognize him as he wore a very formal robe and what could only be described as a judge's wig. It was likely meant to make him appear imposing but he just looked ridiculous, which somehow made me feel slightly more at ease. At least, I did until he barked at me to follow him to the Town Hall.

"I'd like to wait for Ash," I said, looking around at the fences to see if he was there. Some of the other dragons had changed and dressed and were now coming toward us, but there was no sign of him.

"He'll know where you are," replied Spear, catching hold of my arm and pulling me roughly toward the Town Hall.

The other dragons followed. Some I recognized but there were quite a few I'd never seen before.

I was taken through the circular building and into the courtyard. Unlike before when it had been empty, the sandy courtyard was filled with chairs.

"Are we going down to the courtroom?" I asked as Spear dragged me toward the stairs that would lead us down there.

"Not this time. There are too many of us to fit today," he replied brusquely. We came to the small stage where Spear pushed me up the stairs, following close behind.

"Why are we here?" I asked innocently, but I knew. The dragons thought I had tried to escape. That's why so many of them had been flying up on the mountain—to try to find Ash and me.

"My people will not tolerate your behavior. I knew right from the start that having you here would lead to no good. Ash might be blinded by some ridiculous crush, but the rest of us aren't. Thanks to your little escapade last night, I think it's safe to say that you've shown your true colors. You're here, Julianna, to be sentenced to death."

The seats in the courtyard slowly filled up with villagers. They were all here to watch me die.

"I went to my village to find information that will help you!" I cried out.

"Of course you did. Good luck in convincing the court."

I looked out over the almost full courtyard, desperately hoping I'd see Ash in the crowd. It was then that I noticed something that I'd not seen when I'd been there previously—a set of gallows had been erected at the back. They had already made up their minds. I was going to die.

"Ash won't let you do this!" I screamed.

"Ash can't help you now. He's due to be convicted as well."

Ash ran in from the back. No one needed to pull him up onto the stage—he was making his way here all by himself. I felt an immense but misplaced sense of relief on seeing him run up an aisle between the rows of chairs. I wanted to shout out to him, to warn him, but something stopped me. I realized I knew him well enough to know that he wouldn't leave me. Not here and not like this.

"What are you doing? What's going on?" Ash demanded as he stomped to my side.

"I warned you, Ash. You've been brought here to stand before your peers for the crime of treachery. If found guilty, which I can assure you, you will be, you will be hanged."

"Shut it, Spear." Ash took my hand. I felt safer although my situation hadn't improved, just because Ash was by my side. Any safety I felt was just an illusion. There was at least one person guarding each exit, so escape was not an option.

"This is nonsense!" Ash shouted to the assembled crowd. "I admit, we did go to the slayers' village. Julianna took me to her home."

Gasps surrounded me as Ash spoke. I guess everyone thought we were going to deny it.

"She didn't take me there for her benefit, nor for the benefit of her people. She took me there because she thinks that Stone is still alive."

The gasp that I'd heard before was nothing compared to the interested babble that erupted among the crowd.

"It's a lie!" shouted a woman. "I was with him when he died. One of the slayers struck him with his sword. They carried his body down the mountain."

When she stood, I recognized her as the woman that had spoken to Ally the morning after Stone had died.

I couldn't stay quiet any longer. "My people took his body and his soul, but I don't think they took his life. The slayers' swords gain strength with each dragon soul they capture. There is an ancient magic that traps the soul within the sword. I don't understand it myself but I've seen it with my own eyes. My father's sword is one of the most powerful in the whole village. For the longest time, I thought taking a soul meant taking a life, but after hearing Ally speak yesterday about still being able to feel Stone, I believe that Stone might still be alive."

"I can feel him!" I looked to my left. Ally had been sitting in the third row back, but now stood. "I told you all. It makes sense. I knew he was alive."

The sound of the murmuring crowd swelled. They were beginning to question things thanks to Ally. If enough of them believed me, maybe Ash and I would live to see another day after all. The feeling of dread I'd been carrying in my stomach ever since we were escorted here began to dissipate. I didn't want to count my chickens before they hatched, but with Ally on our side, Spear would at least have to consider the fact I was telling the truth.

"If what you say is true, and your people's swords do harbor the souls of our kind, then surely Ally is sensing Stone's soul. Whether his body is dead or alive seems immaterial."

Ally slumped back into his seat as a man in the front row spoke. He was right. How had I not thought of that? The gallows seemed to loom closer as I realized my best defense was completely useless. The best I could hope for was that they believed that I had left the dragon colony in good faith. Judging by the angry faces in the crowd, good faith was in short supply.

"I think we can all agree," began Spear, "that the slayer has acted in a manner that has caused our people grave danger and that Ash has abetted her. The penalty for both of them is death by hanging. I'd like a show of hands of those that believe they are both guilty."

I held my breath as I waited to see if I would live or die. One by one, hands rose. I didn't need to count them to see that a lot more than half the people in the room had deemed us guilty.

It was then that I noticed Edeline for the first time. She sat at the very edge of the courtyard holding on to a very scared looking Lucy. She looked even more terrified at the prospect of us being put to death than I felt. Of course she did. She was about to lose her only son. She'd already lost her husband to my people and now because of the slayers, her eldest child was going to die.

"Wait!"

All eyes turned to Ash. I didn't know what he could say that would get us out of this mess. Whatever it was, I hoped it was good.

"You're sentencing us to die for what? Neither of us has denied going to the village. Did we bring anyone else back here? No. Nor have we brought weapons to hurt anyone here. I've known all of you my whole life, and now you're raising your hands to have me hanged because I took a trip down to the village? It's crazy. If you were so worried that we were bringing the slayers up here, why aren't you out there guarding our town? You all know as well as I do that it's impossible to climb all the way up here. Think about it. What reason do I have for bringing the slayers up here?"

"You might not, but she does," someone shouted out from the back of the hall. Ash's hand tightened around mine.

"Julianna risked her own life last night. She climbed the mountain in last night's storm and attempted to get down to her village in the belief that she could steal a sword to test her theory. She didn't do it for herself. I was with her and I saw with my own eyes the devotion she has shown to the dragons. She even fought her own brother. Her house caught fire. She had to run away, knowing that her home was burning to the ground, and she did all of this for you. You should all be thanking her, not condemning her to death. I'm ashamed of all of you right now, and I'm ashamed to call myself a dragon."

Looks of unease and uncertainty passed through the crowd. Ash had stirred something in them with his speech, but would it be enough to save our lives?

A sharp clap to my left caught my attention. I glanced over to see Ally standing once again, bringing his hands together in applause.

Someone else stood and began to clap. It was Edeline, quickly followed by Lucy. Just as they had raised their hands to condemn us, the rest of the dragons were now standing and applauding us.

Not everyone stood and not everyone joined in, but it was enough to show Spear that they had changed their minds.

"Enough!" Spear strode to the front of the stage and waved his hands to quiet the crowd. Eventually, the clapping stopped. "It seems that your fellow villagers have listened to you. I am not convinced that Julianna knows the truth herself. Her theory has no merit whatsoever beyond Ally thinking his twin is still alive. Denial is a strong part of grief and I believe that Ally is mistaken; however, at this point, we have nothing to lose. I'm not going to send anyone who doesn't want to go to the slayer's village but if anyone wants to volunteer for this fool's errand, then I will not stop you either." He turned to me, anger drawing his brow together. "Once we have gathered the swords, what do you propose we do with them?"

"I don't know," I admitted. After Ash's wonderful speech, I felt pathetic.

"You don't know?" repeated Spear, making me look even more foolish.

"Let's get the swords first," said Ash. "Then we can worry about what to do with them. Who will come with me to the slayer village?"

A small number of people raised their hands. Not as many as those that wanted us dead ten minutes ago, but it was a start.

"Come on!" Ash carried on. "You felt brave enough to kill me by raising your hands five minutes ago. Why not raise your hands again, but this time to show me how brave you really are? These are our ancestors, the trapped souls of our brothers, sisters, mothers, and fathers. Surely that is worth a trip down the mountain!"

A few more hands raised. I started to count them when a flash of light at the back of the room took my attention from them. The gallows had gone up in flames. How was that possible? Had someone set fire to them to save us? The flames rose higher and then the inevitable happened: the thatched roof caught fire. Panic broke out with the people at the back of the courtyard rushing forward to escape the flames. People screamed as the fire quickly engulfed the thatching. Most ran for the exits, though some turned into dragons and flew into the air to escape. Still others turned to protect the ones still in their human forms. Someone grabbed my hand and pulled me through the crowd of terrified people towards the exit.

CHAPTER EIGHTEEN

he heat of the fire became more and more intense as we tried to push our way through the crowd. The whole roof was burning away merrily while chaos reigned in the circle below.

"We aren't going to make it!" I cried to Ash as the fire took hold of the wall beside the exit nearest to us. Ash changed direction, pulling me away from the flames that now surrounded us and into the center of the courtyard. Nearby, someone shifted and flew up into the air.

I grabbed hold of Ash. "Change into a dragon. We can fly out."

"It's not that easy. It takes a lot of energy to shift from one form to another. It's been too long since I last ate or slept. I don't think I can do it."

I had wondered why the others hadn't all shifted into their dragon form and escaped. It would have been easy to fly up and out of harm's way, and yet there were still so many in their human forms wrestling for the doors that would take them outside. Except they wouldn't take them outside. Every door leading away from the courtyard would take them right into the burning building. Anyone trying to escape would have to run through a wall of fire to get through to the other side, and that's if they could even find their way out through the thick blanket of black smoke.

We stood there, just the two of us, right in the center of the chaos. There were still so many people trapped in the courtyard and yet I couldn't see how they would survive if they ran into the burning building. Smoke reached my lungs and I began to cough.

"Do you think we'll survive if we just wait for the building to burn around us?" I asked. Intense heat surrounded us but the walls of the burning building were far enough away to keep the flames from us unless the wind picked up.

"Normally, yes, but the chairs are made out of wood. The ones at the back have already caught fire." Ash guided me away from them, back to the stage.

"We need to make a run for the exits like everyone else then."

"We can't. The others will get through relatively unscathed. As dragons, we can withstand great temperatures, even in our human forms. We cannot withstand fire forever, but all those running for the exits will survive with little damage."

It was because of me that we were trapped. Ash could escape like everyone else, but my human body would burn in the fire. Even if the exits were clear and we could run right through, the chances of me getting through without being badly burned were slim. I couldn't even see the walls now, just a great wall of orange with thick plumes of black smoke billowing into the sky. Most had escaped, either up into the air or through the burning

211

building, but I could still see some stragglers trying to get through the doors. It wouldn't be long until we were the only ones left.

"If you can run through fire—"

"Don't even think it." Ash wrapped his arms tightly around me as if just this small act would shield me from the flames. "I'm not leaving you."

"But you'll die with me."

"Then Spear will get his way."

"Don't say that!"

But he was right. For a second I wondered if Spear had wanted this to happen, had planned it out somehow, but then I remembered the look of shock on his face as the flames took hold, just before he'd changed into his dragon form and flown up into the sky. He could have pulled me up with him and saved me, but he chose not to. He chose to let me die in the flames, but he didn't start them. I tried to think back to what started them, but just as the fire had come from nowhere in my own house, the same had happened here.

"Why would a village of fire-breathing dragons make a town hall out of wood and straw?" I asked feebly. "You were just asking for trouble."

Ash didn't answer, and I didn't expect him to. I couldn't see anyone else now. The flames and their heat were close in every direction. It wouldn't be long before some part of me caught fire, probably my hair and then I'd go up in flames just as the town hall had. Maybe then Ash would be able to escape. The thought gave me a little peace. At least there would be only one casualty in all of this. Ash still had a chance.

I closed my eyes and rested my head on Ash's chest, waiting for the inevitable. A huge gust of cold air made me snap my eyes open. Hot and cold air spun around us as if we were in the center of a small tornado. I couldn't see a thing except for my bright orange hair flapping across my face, mimicking the flames that had surrounded us only moments before. As quickly as it had started, the wind stopped.

I pulled my hair back away from my face to take in the scene before me. The town hall still stood but barely. What was left of the walls was charred black. Wisps of smoke curled into the sky. Most of the chairs were now nothing but ash, although a few closest to us were still intact, showing me just how close the flames had come to us.

The wind came again but this time in a powerful blast as a pair of massive wings flapped, causing my hair to fly out behind me. I shielded my eyes from the soot that blew toward me. The biggest dragon I'd ever seen landed in the center of the ruined courtyard, its wings spanning the entire space. It was green with a tinge of gold glinting in the sun on the tip of every scale.

It folded its wings as its feet touched the ground. I barely had time to comprehend what was happening and how the dragon had seemingly extinguished the flames when the tell-tale sound of bones creaking told me that it was shifting into its human form. I wanted to close my eyes but it was mesmerizing. I'd not seen a dragon shift before and now that I was watching it, I couldn't look away. He shrunk, every part of him seeming to curl up into itself. His snout shortened as his legs lengthened.

The green color warmed until it was the pink of skin. All of this was accompanied by the horrible creaking and squelching sound I'd come to associate with shifting.

Finally, a man stood before us. He was tall and muscular and completely naked. I didn't know where to look.

"Dad!"

Dad? Ash dropped his arms from around me and ran to the man, flinging his arms around him. The man embraced him back.

This was Ash's father? The one who had been killed by a slayer?

He was supposed to be dead! Unless...

Unless my theory was right. I remembered the great green and gold dragon now, Jasper's first kill. I remembered its body being brought down to the village and the big party we had afterward. My mother had remarked on how the dragon's scales glowed in the sunshine.

It was a bizarre scene set out in front of me. The smoldering ruins of the town hall, Ash hugging his naked father. I looked around for something that would cover Ash's dad but almost everything around me was blackened and burned.

Ash's father looked very similar to his son. They had the same thick dark hair and strong jaw line. He was perhaps a couple of inches taller and his shoulders were broader, but it was unmistakable. He opened his eyes. When he noticed me, his expression changed almost immediately. I'd never seen a look of such hatred as the one that Ash's father directed at me now.

CHAPTER NINETEEN

he world seemed to stand still.

"You," he said, "are a slayer."

"Dad, how are you here?" Ash's voice brought me back to reality. A dozen or so of the others had returned, still in their dragon forms. One of them had a blanket in its claws, which it dropped at Ash's father's feet. He picked it up from the floor, wrapping it around himself so he was fully covered. He pulled himself away from Ash, ignoring his son's last question, and strode toward me purposefully.

"You're the reason I'm here. You tried to kill me." His voice was menacing and the speed with which he came towards me made me step back in fear. I'd never seen anyone so angry in my whole life.

"Dad! Stop."

Ash ran forward as his father prodded me in my chest, pushing me back a foot. "Julianna came here to help us. Leave her alone."

Ash's father prodded me again, prompting Ash to pull him back. "No slayer ever helped one of our kind."

"She is helping us."

"Why are you defending her?" He finally took his eyes from me and turned to his son. "Do you have any idea what I've had to endure at the hands of her people? I've been trapped inside a sword for over a year. Do you have any idea what it's like to have your soul taken from your own body and imprisoned in a space as small as that?" He pointed at my sword. "It's cold and dark. I haven't been able to see or feel for over a year. I couldn't speak or hear or move, and yet I could think. I knew I still existed and yet I didn't know how to escape. For a whole year of torment, I was there and yet I was not. If hell exists, I have surely been living it."

"My theory is right." I had thought as much, but to finally hear it from Ash's father's mouth was something else. A small thrill ran through me to know that my friends and family were not murderers at all, but it quickly died when I thought of all those other dragons trapped in the swords, some for decades, even centuries. The thought of being trapped in the darkness for years on end with nothing but my own thoughts horrified me. Maybe death would have been kinder after all.

"What theory?" spat Ash's dad.

"Julianna is one of the slayers, Father, but she didn't know we were shifters. To her, we were nothing more than animals to be hunted."

His father interrupted him. "They know what they are doing. They have always known."

"I didn't. I swear. I knew nothing of your people. I thought of us as hunters and nothing more. Now I see how wrong I was, and I'm sorry."

If I thought my apology would quell his anger, I was wrong. He seemed even more incensed by my words than he had been before.

"You are nothing more than a murderer. Maybe you didn't know that you were trapping our souls, but you cannot tell me that you didn't strike your sword into our bodies to kill us."

"Actually, she didn't kill anyone." Ash stepped in again. "She had the chance to kill me, but instead defended me against her people even before she knew we were shifters. While you can argue that her people did strike to kill us, are we really any better ourselves? We spend our lives training to hunt for meat."

"We hunt to eat, Ash. They hunt for fun, for the glory of the kill. That's what sets us apart from them."

I couldn't defend myself because he was right. We didn't eat the dragons or use their hide for shoes and belts. We killed them and then had a party to celebrate. Shame flooded through me. How had I not seen how sick and utterly pointless it all was? My village was surrounded by bountiful farmlands as far at the eye could see. We were in no danger of starving. If the dragons ever came down to the village to hurt us, perhaps it would have been justified, but yesterday with Ash was the first time I'd ever seen a living dragon in our village.

"You have every right to be angry with me. Ignorance doesn't seem like a very good defense, but it's the only one I have. I can promise you something though. Now that I know about you, I will never slay a dragon, and I'll make it my life's work to stop my people killing yours. I'm glad this has all happened because I would have spent my whole life mindlessly following a path that had been set out for me from birth. I will be blind no more. You have my word."

"Your words mean nothing—"

"Father!" interrupted Ash. He was still holding his father back. "I've been praying for a resolution to the conflict between our people and the slayers. I know that was something you wanted yourself before you went away."

"I was imprisoned."

"Yes, imprisoned, but the fact that you were imprisoned and escaped proves that we can save the others too."

"I want to save the other dragons, sir," I said. "I want to go into my village and let your people go free."

He seemed to calm down a bit while he weighed what I said. Ash finally let him go and he stayed away from me.

Sensing the shift in his mood, I felt safe to ask questions. "How exactly did you escape?" I asked, my voice hesitant but firm. "What was it that let you out of the sword?"

"The last thing I remember before I was trapped was a young man with a group of older men on the mountain. He stabbed me with his sword and at first, I felt pain, but then the pain subsided and there was a kind of whooshing sensation. It was as if I was being sucked out of my own body, and then it all went dark. It was dark ever since, until last night. There was no real sound, but the vibrations made me feel as if something was buzzing around me. Then I sensed movement, the clanging of my sword against another."

"That was me. You were trapped in my brother's sword when I fought him."

"You fought your own brother? Why did you do that?"

"I told you, father, she was fighting him for his sword. She believed that there was the soul of a dragon inside. She wanted to see if it was true."

"You fought for us?" The menacing look dropped from his face and was replaced with something else. If I was to guess, I'd say he was impressed.

"Yes, sir. I wanted to see if I was correct. Now that you are standing here, it seems that I am. Can you tell me what happened after the fight?" I now knew that it was Ash's father that had caused the fire in my house. His escape must have taken so much energy that he'd inadvertently set my house on fire as he left the sword.

"I don't know exactly. It went on for a few minutes and then something changed. It suddenly got very hot. I'd not felt anything for so long that just being able to feel the heat excited me. It meant something was changing. It got hotter until the whooshing sensation happened again. This time it went on for much longer. I felt like I was flying but

223

I had no control. Everything was still dark until I opened my eyes. I was back in my own body. Darkness still surrounded me but this time there were specks of light. It took me a while to realize I was seeing stars and the moon. The ground was soaking wet from rainfall, but I didn't care. I could see and feel and move again. It took a couple of hours for me to readjust to using my body again. I had to relearn how to walk and fly, and by that time dawn had come.

"In many ways, being able to see again was a wonder, but it was also like waking up from one nightmare into another. The bodies of my fellow dragons lay next to mine. I tried waking one I recognized as my uncle's friend who had gone so many years ago. There was the faint beat of his heart, but he didn't stir. I couldn't wake any of them. There were so many dragons there that I knew, all sleeping in some kind of eternal sleep. I had the energy of a newborn, so it took me a long time to get out of there."

"Where were you being kept?" If there was a prison full of sleeping dragons, surely I'd have seen it.

"It was a great place with four large walls but no roof. There was a huge, locked door which I assumed was how we were brought in. I had to fly out over the walls. It was about a mile away from your village, in the forest that borders the Triad Mountains and the farmlands."

I knew where he meant. From the outside, it looked like a castle. I'd asked my father about it and he told me that a giant lived there. I knew he was making it up, but I just assumed it was an old building that was no longer in use. My father had never taken me into that part of the forest again, and as I grew up, I'd forgotten all about it. If only I had known it was full of soulless dragons.

"I spent the morning eating anything I could find. Squirrels, foxes, fruit from the trees. Once I had enough energy, I was able to fly and then I could catch some birds. I flew straight here. When I arrived, I saw that the village was empty of people. It took a few flights over to see everyone in the town hall. I had planned to land outside and change into a man, but I'd forgotten just how much energy that took. I'm afraid I accidentally set fire to the town hall."

"You caused this?"

I turned to see Spear standing behind me. I didn't know how long he'd been there, but he must have come in as a dragon. Unlike Ash's father, he was fully dressed.

"Spear! It's so good to see you." The two men embraced like old friends. "Please forgive me. I can assure you it was entirely accidental."

"No need to apologize, Fiere. It is just good to have you back. I cannot believe my own eyes. My dead best friend standing right in front of me."

"Believe it, Spear."

"I am the only one that owes anyone an apology. I've been wrong, and I can see that now." Spear turned to me. "Julianna and Ash, I hope you'll forgive me. I did not believe you and I did not trust you, and yet you have brought my oldest friend back to me. I thought he was dead. I thought they were all dead."

Someone held my hand. I didn't have to look to know it was Ash.

"I have just one question though," I said. "What made it possible for you to escape? Just fighting with the swords wouldn't have done it. I fought against Jasper and his sword before in training."

"What happened just before the fire started in your house?" asked Ash.

I thought back to the scene from the night before. My father had picked up Jasper's sword and then... and then he had cut my arm.

"It's the blood!" I exclaimed. "My father nicked my forearm, look." I showed them the small cut. "Just after my blood hit the sword, the house caught on fire. If what you said about the intense heat was correct, then it was at that point that your soul left the sword."

"So, it's a dragon's blood that entraps us, but the blood of a slayer that sets us free. There is some poetry in that, would you not agree?" Ash's father said.

I looked at Ash as he looked at me. It seemed that my blood was the key to saving the dragons.

CHAPTER TWENTY

n acrid, burning stench filled my nostrils. Almost without warning, waves of nausea washed over me. The world spun around me and I began to falter. Ash hurried me out of the ruined town hall and back into the village square where we had landed not an hour before. When the fresh air hit my lungs, I immediately felt better, although the underlying nausea was still there, waiting to consume me.

Part of me was elated at figuring out how to save the dragons, but knowing my own blood would have to spill to do it was too much. Just how many dragons were there? My people had been slayers for centuries and I'd lost count of how many dragons had been brought back to the village in just my short lifetime. How much blood would I have to give to save them all? Of course, if it was just a tiny drop and if it was just my blood, I might feel okay about it, but it wasn't just a small drop. When my father had nicked me with his sword, the cut had been superficial but quite a bit of my blood had hit the sword. Multiply that by the hundreds, or even thousands, of dragon souls we had stolen and I wouldn't have any blood left in my body. The dragons would have to use the blood of my family, of my friends.

"Are you okay?" Ash gently placed his fingers under my chin and lifted it until I was looking at him. I couldn't lie to him.

"Not really."

"We'll figure all this out, don't worry."

"Don't worry?" Easy for him to say. He didn't have a hoard of dragons wanting to take all his blood. I shivered despite the warmth of the air.

"I'm not going to let anyone hurt you if that's what you're thinking. It can't only be your blood that works. There must be other's blood we can use instead."

I knew he meant well, but using other's blood was exactly what I was afraid of. Still, his arms around me were comforting, and just for a minute, I enjoyed his warmth and tried to forget about what I knew was coming.

It didn't last long. The dragons who had followed us had changed and dressed, including Fiere.

A couple of women brought chairs and tables from one of the cafes that lined the square. A neighboring restaurant did the same, bringing enough chairs for everyone to sit on. Ash took my hand and led me to one of the tables. Almost as soon as we sat, a waitress brought us both a cup of coffee and a slice of cake each. Spear sat to one side of me, making me feel nervous. The others had all changed into their human forms and joined the impromptu party or meeting.

Suddenly, a loud scream made me jump and spill my coffee all over the table. Edeline ran towards us, tears in her eyes and arms outstretched. Lucy was just behind her, her small legs struggling to keep up with her mother. Edeline jumped into Fiere's arms, burying her head in his shoulder. Seconds later Lucy barged into them and was enveloped into the hug.

"You should go to them," I said to Ash. His back turned to me as he went back to his family. A pang of sadness hit me as I wondered what my own family was doing right now and if they were out looking for me.

"As many of you can see, our brother Fiere has returned to us," began Spear, standing to address the others. "I owe you all an apology. Julianna was telling the truth. Our ancestor's souls have been trapped by the slayer's swords but their living bodies remain, hidden in a secret place outside of the slayer village. Julianna's own blood is the key to releasing our people, and it is because of her that Fiere is back. The fire that destroyed the town hall was an accident and I know that Fiere wouldn't mind me telling you that it was he who started it. After so long trapped inside a sword, he's not quite used to being back in his body. I'm sure no one will hold that against him."

"I'm sorry everyone," said Fiere, finally extracting himself from his family. Ash came to sit next to me with his family on his other side. Lucy perched on her father's lap.

A cheer went up as I looked around me; a sea of smiling faces greeted me, glad to have one of their own back. I lifted the corners of my mouth to join in, but the thought of what my people and I would have to do to free all the dragons was a constant thought in my mind.

"What about Stone?" Ally shouted. "Did you see him? Is he still alive?"

"I'm afraid when I woke up I was very weak. I saw many dragons and tried to wake the ones nearest to me, but I can't remember who I saw. There were many, many of our people there. I'm sure Stone will be among them."

"I knew he was alive. I knew it!" Ally's fist pumped the air, his joy evident for all to see. "We need to go and get him."

"We need to go into the slayer village and rescue all of them," said Spear. "Most of you here have lost someone to the slayers so I think you'll agree with me; however, it's not just a case of flying into the village and waking our brethren. We have to get the swords first. Only then will we be able to save the dragons. We need to make a plan."

"How will we find all the swords?" asked a man I hadn't seen before.

"It's good that we have someone who knows the village very well." Spear's hand clapped heavily on my shoulder, pushing me down in my chair. If only he'd pushed a bit harder, I could have disappeared under the table completely. "Julianna has agreed to help us. She'll be able to tell us where the swords are and who owns them. She is a valuable resource indeed. With her help, we can make a map of the village and write up profiles on the owners of the swords."

Everyone began to clap again, this time for me. I picked up my cup and managed a weak smile. I'd said I'd help the dragons but I'd not mentioned anything about maps or profiles. I wanted to help the dragons and see the same look of joy on their faces that were currently being shown by Edeline and Lucy, but to do that, I'd be betraying my own kind.

"With Julianna's help, we'll know the slayer village intimately. We will know at what time everyone gets up and what time they go to bed, what time they eat and who goes to work where. I'm not going to send anyone down to the village until we're ready."

"But I want to go fetch my brother now," Ally said in protest. "He needs me."

"He does need you, but he needs you not to get caught. You will be of no use to him if you end up trapped too."

"So what?" replied Ally, standing. "I'd rather be trapped with him than sitting around here drinking coffee and eating cake."

"Fine, you go to him now, but which sword was it that took him? Because if you end up trapped in a different sword, you'll be even further from being reunited with him than you are now."

Ally sat down, defeated.

"Does anyone else want to start their own crusade, or are we going to do what we always do and work as a team?"

No one spoke.

"That's what I thought. Now here's what I propose. First of all, we need our strongest and most able men and women to go and fight."

I winced at the word fight.

A number of hands shot up into the air, Ally's among them.

"I also need volunteers to help rebuild the town hall. Those of you offering to fight can start on that until we have our maps and plans. With Julianna helping us, they shouldn't take too long to write up, maybe a couple of days. Just how many swords do you think we'll need to look for?"

Ash nudged me when I didn't answer. Was Spear talking to me?

How many swords were we looking for? That was a tricky question. Almost everyone had a sword in Dronios. Receiving one was a rite of passage. I tried adding up just how many swords there were in the village. There must be at least a hundred.

Granted, many of the villagers didn't use them and instead had them showcased in frames on their walls, but all of them at one point would have had to come up the mountain on their eighteenth birthday. Of course, there were also swords like my father's that had been used on many dragons, though I couldn't say exactly how many.

"I would say there are between eight and fifteen swords you'll need to find first. Not everyone in Dronios slays dragons, but there is a group of men who are up the mountain more than anyone else, the elders of our village. It's these men who will have most of your people trapped in their swords."

I felt like enough of a betrayer just telling them this snippet of information, so I could hardly tell them that they would need to target most of the people in town as well. My own father was one of the men in the group I'd mentioned. If he knew I was telling the dragons about him, he'd probably never speak to me again. At least not until he knew the truth about them, that they were shifters. My father was many things, but he wasn't a murderer. I knew he'd never take the life of another person. I hoped he'd find it in his heart to understand what I was trying to do and to forgive me because of it.

"It seems Julianna is now our biggest ally. I'll work with her closely over the coming days to define a plan that will allow us to free the dragons."

"Didn't you say that it was Julianna whose blood we would have to use to free them?" someone shouted.

I'm glad someone had noticed because Spear seemed to have skated over that small piece of information. Ash gripped my hand tightly under the table.

"Well, yes," said Spear, giving a little cough. "That's something to worry about further down the line. Today our priority is to make a plan and find the swords. As for the freeing of the dragon's souls, we can cross that bridge when we come to it."

"But we will need to use her blood, right? Why would she do that? She is a Slayer," the man pushed.

They were speaking over me as if I wasn't even there. A waitress refilled my coffee and handed me another slice of cake on a stone plate even though I'd not touched the first one.

"Well, as I've already said, she's agreed to help us. Isn't that right, Julianna?

All eyes turned to me. It was all well and good, Spear telling everyone I would help, but now that he was asking me to agree with him, I had to make a decision. On one hand, I wanted nothing more than to help these people, to return their lost loves to their community, but I knew that in doing so, my own people might be hurt. Having a plan was a good idea, but plans weren't infallible.

I thought of my father then, how he had been so proud of me on my last day of being seventeen. Was that really only a week ago? It felt like a lifetime. If I said yes to them, he would forgive me, right? All through Spear's speech, I'd been thinking of my family and how they had always taught me right from wrong, but doing the right thing now could hurt them all. They might never forgive me, and in that case, I might never see them again. It was breaking my heart, and yet how could I leave so many dragons trapped, knowing that I was the only one that could save them? I'd never be able to live with myself.

I took a deep breath, ready to utter the words that would change not just my life, but the lives of everyone, dragon and slayer alike

Ash's hand gripped mine hard. His emerald eyes glistened as he nodded at me. It was an almost imperceptible tilt of the head meant just for me, but I saw it and knew what it meant. He wasn't asking me to agree like Spear was. He was giving me his support to make up my own mind. He understood the position I was in as no one else did. Everyone was so keen to bring back their loved ones that any thoughts of my welfare and that of my family had not even been a consideration. Ash was different though. He looked at both sides of the issue and had an empathy I was yet to find in any other person or dragon. I knew Ash would support me in whatever decision I made, and for that I was grateful. That was also what led me to the decision I was about to make.

CHAPTER TWENTY-ONE

es." There, I'd said it. "I'll help you. I'll help you find the swords but I have one condition."

Spear smiled. "And what condition is that my dear?"

"I want no harm to come to the people of my village. If we do this, we do it in peace."

"Are you proposing we fly down to Dronios and ask them nicely to give us their swords?"

A couple of the people in the crowd giggled.

"No, of course not," I replied feeling annoyed. "What I'm saying is that we do this at night without making a fuss."

Because that had gone so well last time. At least this time I had a couple of days to plan it.

Hopefully, if I did a good job, we could retrieve the swords without making the same mistakes as last time.

"Of course. None of us wants anyone to get hurt but we must also be realistic. Even the best-laid plans can fail as you yourself discovered the other night."

"Now that I know that blood is the answer, I know not to bleed on any of the swords until they are safely away." The last thing I needed was to destroy any more of the village with fire.

"I'm sure that you didn't intend to bleed on the last sword, but you did."

"That's true, but it won't happen again." Of course, I couldn't know that for sure, but I was certainly planning to keep my blood in my own body for as long as possible.

"Let's hope so for all of our sakes."

Spear was really beginning to annoy me with his condescending attitude. I wanted to tell him to go shove it but I knew I couldn't. I'd already committed to helping them out.

"So," carried on Spear to the rest of the crowd, "those of you who have volunteered to go down into Dronios must do their level best not to do anything that might get anyone hurt. I know that retribution must be in all your minds as you fly down the mountain and that after centuries of them murdering our people, you'll want to have your revenge, but you must keep this instinct in check."

"That's not fair!" I shouted, standing up and knocking over my second cup of coffee. The waitress immediately ran over to mop up the spill. "My people are not murderers!"

"How do you explain all of our people that have been murdered by yours then?"

He had such a smug smirk on his face, I had half a mind to punch him in it. I didn't want to point out that not a single dragon had been murdered, just imprisoned within the swords. He already knew that; he was just baiting me.

"My people didn't know you were shifters. Had they known, we would have let you be. We thought the dragons were a threat to our safety. That is why we became slayers."

"Slayers. Yes, such an interesting term for a girl who doesn't think of herself as a murderer."

"Spear," Ash stood, matching my own indignation. "You've gone too far. You know as well as I do that Julianna isn't a murderer. Hasn't the fact that she's just agreed to help you been enough proof for you?"

"Maybe not," replied Spear, "but she's wrong about her people not knowing. Maybe she's just ignorant of it, but her people have always known."

I didn't like being called ignorant, but the alternative was worse—that my family and I had always known about the dragons being shifters and I was lying about it.

"I am not ignorant and I'm not lying. I know my family and I know my friends. They would never harm another soul." I was still shouting and I didn't care. I was the only one here that could defend my people.

"Interesting choice of words considering that's exactly what your people have been doing for centuries. I didn't mean to call you ignorant, but the fact of the matter is, the slayers have known about us being shifters for centuries. There's a book about it in the library here in town that I'm sure we can check out."

"Maybe it's a work of fiction?" I tried desperately, sitting back down in my seat. Another cup of coffee had magically appeared on the table in front of me. I had to be careful not to spill this one.

"It's called The History of Frokontas. Does that sound like a work of fiction to you?"

He directed the question at me but didn't wait for an answer. Not that I was planning on giving him one anyway.

"In the book, there is a whole chapter about the slayers. It is said that there was a meeting way back when between the elder from Dronios and the elder from Frokontas. They sat with each other and discussed their differences. It was made very clear to your elder at the time that we were shifters and that we were a peace-loving people, but your elder refused to cease slaying. He said it was all his people had ever known and they would keep fighting us until there wasn't a dragon left in the sky."

"That can't be!" I cried out. Surely the book was wrong. I looked to Ash for support, but he only whispered that he'd read the book too.

"Let's be clear on one thing, Julianna. Humans have always had a deep mistrust of shifters. From the battles of the wolves in the north to the war of the sea-shifters in the east, humans have never let us be. Where there is a community of shifters, there is a settlement of humans who believe it is their destiny to destroy them. Your village is no different."

He was right, but how could he possibly be? He'd used practically the same words my father had said to me—that it was our destiny to destroy them. How could my father have known? How could he have kept this from me, his own flesh and blood, his own daughter? I remembered the words he said to me the day before my birthday. After today you will know everything there is to know about being a slayer. You will learn our secrets.

At the time, I thought he was talking about learning to fight, but maybe he was going to tell me that the dragons were shifters. Maybe he knew all along. Jasper knew too. I remembered how haughty he had been about me not knowing everything.

They were going to tell me after my first kill. Once I'd already killed a dragon—or thought I had—it would have been too late to back out. I'd already be a murderer. The memory of all those parties came back to me. All the times we danced around the body of a dragon and celebrated the kill. They had known that it was a person. How could anyone do that, let alone a whole village? And they must have known. Everyone killed a dragon on their eighteenth birthday. There were few exceptions. Many didn't carry on in the pursuit of killing them, but almost everyone had blood on their hands. The thought made me sick.

I stood up quickly and ran into the café bathroom. Once there, I retched but nothing came up. Looking in the bathroom mirror while washing my hands, I wasn't surprised to see I'd been crying.

My eyes were red-rimmed and salty tears had left tracks down my grimy face. I'd not even felt the tears falling. Perhaps I was in shock.

Someone knocked at the bathroom door.

"Julianna? Are you ok?" It was Ash.

"Not really." I splashed water on my face before stepping out of the bathroom. As soon as I'd closed the door behind me, he enveloped me into a soothing hug. I hated him seeing me like this again, all sad and misty-eyed. I'd been brought up as a warrior, not a cry baby.

"My whole life has been a lie. I swear I never knew."

"I know, Julianna. I've already told you I believe you. Whether your ancestors knew is another matter."

I pulled back and looked him in the eye. "You say ancestors as though they all died long ago. We're talking about my father, my mother, everyone! Is what Spear said the truth?"

"I've read the book he talked about. Everyone here has. We don't have school here like you do, but we're taught by our parents from a young age, and that book is the most frequently checked out book from the library."

"I can't believe it. I just can't."

"I don't know what's true and what isn't. That book was written a long time ago about a conversation that happened a long time before that. Stories change over time. What's to say this one didn't? For all we know, the two elders were drinking mead together and having a good time like old friends. It doesn't sound too dramatic now, does it?" Ash shrugged his shoulders. "The author had to add some excitement in there so he fabricated a fight."

I punched him playfully on the shoulder. "You're just teasing me."

"I wanted to see you smile, that's all."

"What now?" Outside, Spear appeared to have moved on to some other topic as he gestured wildly at the burned remains of the building.

"Now we carry on with our plan."

"To get the swords?"

"Yes, that is important. We need our people back, but that is Spear's plan. Our plan is to make the dragons and the slayers see eye to eye."

I sighed. "I don't think that's going to happen in a hurry. Not if what Spear said is true."

"When my dad was taken from us, I was so angry. I wanted to go down the mountain and burn all your houses and hurt as many of you as I could."

"What stopped you?" I was fascinated to hear this. It didn't seem like Ash at all.

"Lucy. She asked me what that would solve and I realized she was right. It would solve nothing. Killing your people wouldn't bring my father back; it would just make the slayers angrier so they would come after more dragons. It was a self-perpetuating circle of hate, and I decided right there to break it. Of course, I could only think and act for myself, not for others, so the hate continued, but I've tried very hard to make the dragons see both sides of the story and not just what they want to see."

I looked at him and realized how brave he was. I wouldn't have been able to do the same if I were in his position.

I leaned forward, full of a need I'd not known before and brushed his lips with mine. This was nothing like the small peck I'd given him all those days before on the training ground with Stone and Ally. This was a kiss brought about by a fear of my past and a yearning to be with another person who understood what I was going through. I was aware that I was using the kiss to take away my pain, but perhaps it would take away some of his too. The intensity of the feelings rushing through me took me by surprise as our lips worked together. When he eventually pulled back, I knew that for both our sakes, the plan had to work.

"Come on. We should go back outside. They'll be wondering where we are."

"Can't we just stay in here forever?" I asked, only half-joking, but I knew we couldn't. Sooner or later, we'd have to go back to reality.

Chapter Twenty-Two

o give Spear his due, he didn't make any mention of my sudden disappearance. The talk had turned very animated in my absence and it seemed they were discussing how the new town hall should look.

"I'll tell you everything you need to know, but we have to do it now." I didn't want to give myself time to change my mind.

Everyone stopped talking and, not for the first time, all eyes were on me.

"Okay then," said Spear, looking directly at me. "I think we should discuss this somewhere a little less crowded. You can come to my house. Those of you that have agreed to go to the slayer village can come with us. Everyone else, thank you for your input, but I think we should adjourn this meeting here."

The sound of a hundred chairs being pulled back all at once filled the air. A group of people walked over to Spear. Ally was among them, as was the girl who had been with Stone at the time of his soul being taken. I didn't recognize the rest apart from Lucy, who had pulled away from Edeline and Fiere.

"I think you are a little too small to fight, Lucy," Ash said with a grin, ruffling her hair.

"Fight? Who said anything about fighting?" I asked, feeling nervous at what I was about to do.

"You know what I mean," he said to me. To Lucy, he said, "Go with Mom and Dad. I'll be home later."

"I can fight!" she said, pulling herself up to her full height which wasn't much. She placed her hands on her hips and looked at her older brother with indignation.

He kissed her lightly on the cheek. "I know you can, but we want to give the slayers a chance, don't we?"

I knew he was joking, but his words made my stomach churn.

"You've not seen Dad in a year. I have to go to this meeting because Julianna needs me, but Dad would be awfully upset if neither of his children was there for his homecoming."

She seemed to weigh it in her mind, then jogged back to her parents.

"Sorry about how I phrased it. I hope there won't be any fighting, but she's so young and doesn't really know what's going on. It was easier to word it like I did than explain."

"Surely that's precisely the reason we're in this mess in the first place?" I ventured.

"Okay, everyone," began Spear, not leaving Ash time to respond. "Let's go."

Frokontas was a small place so it didn't take long until we were at Ash's house on the opposite end of town. There were quite a few farms and pretty houses dotted around the landscape, but it didn't take a genius to guess which one belonged to Spear.

It was the largest house in the whole town and the only one that had more than two stories. Made out of white painted wood, it rose from the ground like a monolith. On the very top was a landing pad, but it was not there that we entered. Instead, we walked up a tree-flanked walkway to a huge door that must have been ten feet tall.

"It's so I can entertain people in their dragon form," he explained as he opened the door. "I don't like people coming in from the top and going through my house."

I followed him into a huge hallway with a polished floor and a wide, sweeping staircase.

A woman in a smart white uniform appeared. "Sir, can I get you anything?"

"Just bring some lemonade into the parlor, please. I think we've all had enough coffee to last a lifetime."

She curtsied and left through the door she had come from.

The parlor was a huge room with large windows that made it much brighter than the entrance hall had been.

Even though there were about twenty of us, we all found somewhere to sit comfortably on the sofas that were spread around the room.

"So," I began, feeling nervous. What I was about to do was a betrayal to my whole family. I cleared my throat and started again. "So, the swords. Everyone in Dronios gets one on their eighteenth birthday. They're all unique, although they all look similar to mine." I held my sword aloft for them to see.

"This one is light because it has never killed another being or taken a soul. Essentially, it's just a piece of hollow metal."

"You make your swords hollow?" someone asked. "Surely that would make them weaker."

"These are special swords. Yes, they are hollow. They need to be to hold souls but don't make the mistake of thinking that weakens them. They are imbibed with goblin magic."

"The goblins make them?" he asked, impressed now.

I knew why. Anything made by goblins was expensive. They mined the metal in the Triad Mountains and put their own magic into everything they made. Those that could afford it invariably ordered magic crowns, necklaces or other jewelry, but the slayers decided that was a waste of magic long ago and commissioned swords instead. Each one cost as much as a house in Dronios, but it was worth it. If a slayer lost their sword, they'd never be able to afford another one.

"Yes, so you can understand that this isn't going to be easy. Now I know that I said everyone in the village over the age of eighteen had a sword. That's true, but there are also others. When a person dies, their sword is deemed too special to give to someone else so they're put in the village stronghold."

"That's fine. We'll just go in there after we've found the other swords," said Ash.

"Not quite. I don't know where it is. I only know it exists because my mother told me that my grandfather's sword was put in there when he died ten years ago."

"This is going to be much harder than I imagined," said Spear. He'd not sat down yet but was instead pacing the room while I spoke. "We need a map. How are your drawing skills?"

He didn't wait for me to answer before unrolling a length of parchment on a table at the edge of the room and handing me a pot of ink and a quill.

I closed my eyes, trying to picture just how my village would look from above. On the far left of the paper, I drew a small square to symbolize my house. Of course, that had been burnt down, and I didn't know where my family was staying, but I felt that I should put it on the map anyway. If the dragons were flying in, they'd need to get the full picture. To the right, I drew the track that led to the heart of the village and a big circle to denote the center, with five houses around it. Then, to the far right, I drew another house. There were others of course, but as I drew the map, it occurred to me that only seven of them mattered. The seven I'd drawn in belonged to the founding families of the village and the only ones that were really considered slayers. In each building, I put a large cross, before filling in another few houses.

"What do the crosses mean?" Spear asked, looking over my shoulder.

"Dronios is a slayer village, but that doesn't mean that everyone in the village is a slayer. There are seven main families in the village. These are the ones that have swords, or at least the ones that have swords like mine. I've marked a cross in the houses where I know there will be the most valuable sword."

"Ok, seven families. Got it. Can you write the number of swords in each household next to it on the map? That way, we'll have a good idea what we're up against."

I nodded my head. Next to my house, I wrote the number four before crossing it out and writing three. I'd forgotten for a second that I had my own sword with me. Next to it, I drew a question mark.

"This is my house," I explained to Spear. "It burned down the other night and I don't know where my family is."

I was just about to write a five beside the next house when the maid bustled in with a large try of cups and a jug of lemonade.

"I'm afraid we 'e using the table, so you'll all have to pour your own lemonade and pass the jug around." Spear turned back to the chart.

I mentally added up everyone in the village and wrote the numbers in.

"Thirty-three," said Spear adding the numbers. "There are thirty-three people in your village with slayer swords?"

"Thirty-four," I replied, indicating mine. "Mine is the only empty one though. As I've only just turned eighteen, mine is the newest in the village. You've got to remember the ones that were owned by my ancestors though. I have no way of knowing just how many there are." I drew another box at the top of the paper and put a large question mark in it. Underneath I wrote "Stronghold."

"Wonderful, Julianna," Spear said, pulling the paper out from under my hands. "This will help immensely."

He held it up for the others to see as I sat beside Ash.

"There are thirty-three swords to find, plus some more in a stronghold. Julianna doesn't know where this is but I'm sure we will be able to find it. I say we go in tonight and grab the swords under the cover of darkness. If you could all—"

"I thought you were going to wait a couple of days?" I asked, interrupting him. "Weren't you going to make a start on building the new town hall?"

"The town hall can wait. This is more important."

"No!" I shouted although I didn't know why. I'd agreed to this. It had to happen sooner or later. Did it really matter what day they went down?

And yet, the thought of my mother popped into my head. My dear, sweet mother who wouldn't hurt a fly. Sure, she was from a long line of slayers, but she had problems killing a chicken for dinner. She always had to get my father to do it for her. There was no way she would be able to knowingly kill another person, even if they were dragon shifters.

"Can't we just go to the village and ask them to give us the swords?" Even as I said it I knew it sounded lame.

Some of the people laughed and my cheeks reddened.

"I don't think that's an option, Julianna. Maybe you should go home with Ash now and let us plan for this evening."

"No, you need my help," I insisted. And I needed to be there to make sure that no one was going to get hurt.

"And you have helped. This map is invaluable to us."

"You can't just go blundering into my village. Someone will get hurt."

"She's right, Spear," said Ash "Thirty-three swords is a lot to find in one night, not to mention the ones in the stronghold. Why not just go and find some of them tonight and do the rest later?"

"Actually, that's not a bad idea. It will make it easier. We'll attack just these houses tonight," he said, pointing to two of the houses in the village.

"You can't attack anyone," I objected. "The men hold their swords close by because of the power they hold. You won't be able to do it without me."

"Attack was probably too strong a word. I want no casualties on either side, but I will get the swords. If they put up a fight, we will win. You should never underestimate the power of a dragon. Please take her home, Ash. Now."

"I'm not going," I stated, but Ash took hold of my arm.

"Come on. We may as well go home. I've not seen Dad in a year and I want to be home for the celebration."

I wanted to stay, but how could I ask him to stay with me when the father he previously thought was dead was at home waiting for him?

As I left the room, I heard them discussing their plans without me. The thought of them going to my village without me with information that I had given them made me feel sick.

"Why did you make me leave?" I asked once we were out of the house.

264

"Because I know Spear. If we didn't go, and you kept trying to undermine him, he'd have locked you up somewhere. It's better that we leave now while you're still free and come up with a plan of our own."

I already had a plan. I'd been thinking about it since Spear had told everyone that they would be attacking my village tonight. I was going to go there before him. I was going to tell my family the truth. Once they knew that the dragons were shifters, they'd hand their swords over to me.

At least, I hoped they would.

CHAPTER CWENTY-CHREE

'd felt like an outsider many times since coming to Frokontas, but this was the first time I'd felt like that in Ash's home.

Edeline had prepared a huge dinner for Fiere to welcome him home, and even though I was invited to join them, I didn't want to interrupt the family reunion, so I took my plate and ate in my room.

My mind kept going over everything that had happened over the last few hours. I shouldn't have told Spear about my village, at least not until I knew for sure that I would be allowed to go too. It was too late now though. He'd made his plans and I wasn't a part of them. I cursed myself for letting it come to this, but what choice did I really have? I couldn't let my people keep killing the dragons knowing they were shifters. I wrestled with my conscience all evening, indecisive about what I should do. I could leave the dragons. Attempt one last time to reason with my family. Warn them what was coming and how to stop it. If they relinquished their swords, all would be over.

I'd made up my mind by the time I heard the family going to bed. I was going to sneak out. Okay, I'd tried once before and ended up lost in a maze deep within the mountains, dripping wet and freezing cold, but this time I'd go prepared. When the house was quiet, I tiptoed downstairs into the kitchen. There, I took a torch and some chalk I'd seen earlier on Lucy's desk to mark my way on the tunnel walls. I also took Edeline's heavy coat and threw it over my tunic. The only armor I carried was my sword, which I hoped I wouldn't have to use.

"I knew you'd try this again."

I jumped as I turned to find Ash staring at me from the other side of the kitchen.

"I have to go."

"You promised me that you'd always tell me. I don't want you getting lost in the mountains again. You know I'm coming with you, right?"

"That's why I didn't tell you. I knew you'd want to come and I didn't want to put you in the position of choosing between me and your family."

"Isn't that the choice you have to make?" Ash arched his eyebrow at me. "Julianna, we're a team. We're in this together. There are going to be difficult decisions that we will face, but if we don't confide in one another, we'll have to do it alone. Now go back upstairs."

"Go upstairs? I'm not going back to bed." I stomped my foot in agitation.

"And I'm not asking you to. We're going to fly and the best place to take off from is the balcony outside of your room."

With a nod, I turned and once again tiptoed through the house. He was right of course. The balcony was the perfect place to fly from. Ash quickly shifted into his mighty red dragon and I jumped onto his back as he spread his wings and we took to the sky. It was so much nicer flying up the mountain as opposed to walking up the stone steps in a storm. The evening was calm and quiet, quite the opposite of how I felt. Normally I'd enjoy the feeling of weightlessness as we soared through the air, but my stomach churned as I thought about what I'd have to face in Drionos.

Last time we were both there, my family hadn't given me the chance to explain. They'd taken one look at Ash and attacked. Having him with me again might not be the best idea, but this time I would make them listen to us. I wondered just how badly our house had been burned, if they had somehow managed to control the flames or if it had burned down completely. Just thinking about it brought tears to my eyes.

We flew over the peak of the mountain, this time not bothering with any tunnels. It was a clear night with a bright moon. The mountains looked stunning bathed in pale moonlight, but I couldn't focus my attention on them too long. I wanted to see what had happened to my house. I strained my eyes into the distance, trying to see if it was still standing, but it was only when we came to land in the village that I finally saw the extent of the devastation. I threw Ash's clothes at him and waited for him to transform. We'd landed on the path at the edge of the village and my house, or what was left of it, was nothing but a silhouette in the distance. I could see enough to know that no one could possibly be living there anymore.

"It's gone," I said when Ash was back in his human form.

"It's too far away to know that. There is still a building there. Maybe it isn't as bad as you think."

I set off up the path at a brisk pace, hopeful that Ash could see something that I was missing and not just the burned shell that used to be my home. He did have much better eyesight than I did, especially in the dark.

As we got closer, it became obvious that I was right and that Ash was wrong. There wasn't a building there, just a blackened frame where there used to be one.

"I'm sorry," Ash whispered, pulling me into a hug. His wide arms comforted me. "It was the barn

I saw back there, not the house. I confused the two."

I looked over to the barn. Thankfully it was far enough away from the house to not have sustained any damage.

Fear enveloped me and my breathing became ragged. I'd been trying so hard not to cry that I was overcome by a panic attack instead. I tried to regulate my breathing and get it down to a normal speed.

"Julianna," Ash spoke calmly and quietly. "We'll find them. You saw yourself that they escaped. Wherever they are, they're safe."

I nodded. He was right. I'd seen them all leave the burning building, but where were they now? I didn't know where to begin to look.

"Who's that?" a voice shouted, making me jump. "I can hear you whispering, so don't try to pretend you're not there."

I looked over to see Jasper with a lantern. He'd obviously come from the barn. So that's where they were living. I felt a little relieved. The barn was safe and warm and would be cozy with all the hay.

"Jasper, it's me." I moved into the light, pulling Ash with me.

His eyes grew wide and his hand automatically went to his side where he usually kept his sword in a sheath, except he wasn't wearing it. By the way he was dressed, I guessed we had woken him up.

"I don't want to fight you," I said, taking a step toward him with my hands held in front of me.

He stepped back toward the barn door.

"Father!" he shouted, not taking his eyes from us. My father's bulky frame appeared at the door.

"What is it?"

"I told you it wasn't dogs. It's her...with him." He spat the last word out.

"Julianna?" My mother's hopeful voice sounded out and before either Jasper or my father could react, she ran over to me, her arms outstretched.

She was so tiny compared to me and yet I felt so safe in her arms. We both burst into tears as she hugged me tightly.

"Julianna, who is this and why have you brought him here again? Didn't he cause enough damage the last time?" My father sneered.

"Stay back, Elgin," my mother shouted. "This is our little girl, remember? Not one of your dragons. Don't even think about getting your sword out."

I'd never heard her stand up to my father before and I wasn't sure who was more surprised, me or my father.

"You'd better come in and you can bring your...friend."

"Thanks, Mom."

They'd done a good job with the barn. Someone had given them blankets which they'd laid on the hay for beds and seating. A couple of lanterns lit up the place, making it feel warm although I couldn't help thinking it was another fire waiting to happen.

I sat on a bale of hay with Ash beside me. My family sat opposite us. Jasper had a sullen look about him.

"Come back to do more damage, have you?" he asked, looking straight at Ash. "Or are you just here to kidnap someone else?"

"I wasn't kidnapped!" I replied.

"Of course you weren't. I can see that," said my mother before turning to Jasper. "And any more silly remarks like that and you can sleep outside."

Jasper pouted and folded his arms.

"Can you tell us what did happen to you? I've been worried sick."

My heart went out to my mother. I could see the worry lines etched onto her face and I hated that it was because of me that they were there.

"When Papa and Jasper last saw me on the hunting trip, I fell and Ash caught me. He wasn't kidnapping me. He was saving me."

"That's a lie. She was taken by a dragon. I saw it carry her off. This guy must have killed the dragon and then kidnapped her," said Jasper, not heeding my mother's warning.

"Ash didn't kill the dragon." I entwined my hands in his. I needed his strength now with what I was about to say. "Ash is the dragon."

I proceeded to tell them about Frokontas and the dragon shifter community there. My mother listened intently, although I could see the shock on her face. Even Jasper had been rendered mute with the revelation.

"I tried telling you all this before when I came down the mountain, but—"

Jasper sneered. "But you attacked me with your sword and set fire to the house instead."

"Jasper, I'm warning you!" My mother gave him a look of disgust.

"You attacked me if you remember, but that's another thing. The fire started when the dragon enslaved in the sword escaped. When you nicked my arm, Papa, my blood set off a magical reaction in the sword, allowing the soul of the dragon inside it to be free. It was not the fault of the dragon, but of the magic. This reaction was so fierce and full of energy that it sparked, setting the house on fire."

"That's preposterous," replied Jasper. "How do you even know that? It sounds made up."

"I know because I've spoken to that dragon. That dragon is Ash's father. His soul has been trapped in that sword since you slay it. When he was released, his soul went back to his body. There's a place somewhere in the forest where the

276

soulless dragons lie. You didn't kill a dragon on your birthday. No one has killed a dragon. Instead, their souls are captured and taken into the swords to make them stronger."

"We've always known the dragons' souls end up in our swords, that doesn't mean they aren't dead." Jasper's eyes narrowed in a mixture of confusion and anger.

"They aren't dead. Ash's dad saw them. He says it's like they are asleep. What we're doing is barbaric and needs to be stopped. I've come today to ask you for your swords. We need to free the dragons because they're people, not animals for slaughter."

"Oh, my!" My mother put her head in her hands.

"What you're saying makes no sense. If we have their souls, why keep them alive?" Jasper shook his head, still not believing me.

"I don't know. Maybe they have to be alive somewhere to make the magic work."

"You aren't having my sword," Jasper said stubbornly. "If what you say is true, which I sorely doubt, then it's empty anyway."

"How can you doubt it? Surely you've felt the loss of power from it since the night the house burned down. You must have wondered why."

"I've not used it since then. I was waiting for you to bring this guy back so I could use it on him."

"Jasper, I've had enough. If you can't be civil, you can sleep outside with the cattle."

Jasper scowled, but he didn't dare disobey our mother. He picked up his sword and left, slamming the barn door behind him.

"Papa," I turned to my father, who hadn't said a word. "You are the greatest slayer in the village. I'm not going to ask if you know anything about the dragons being kept alive, because how could you not know, but I know you wouldn't have done this if you knew that the dragons were people. I need your sword. I need to set them free. Will you please give it to me?"

He stood and picked up his sword. "I love you my daughter, but I cannot give you my sword."

"Why ever not?" my mother asked. "She's told you why she needs it. I can't bear the thought of all those people trapped in there. We need to let them out."

"I captured those souls fair and square. They belong to me."

"But they're people!"

"I know they're people. I've always known they were people."

"You knew?" I asked my father, barely believing what he was telling me.

"Of course I knew. Just because they are people doesn't mean they aren't a nuisance. They're still dragons, too, and dragons kill people."

"No, they don't! When was the last time you remember a slayer being killed by a dragon from the Triad Mountains?"

"There have been times."

"Not many, and only then because we were trampling around up there waving our swords around. If they killed, it was only in self-defense."

"Enough!" shouted my father. "We have worked hard to keep this village safe from those dragons and this is how you repay me? By coming here and telling me to give up my sword? If you want my sword, you will have to fight me for it!" He growled and pierced Ash with his heated gaze.

Chapter Twenty-Four

I looked up at my father, barely able to comprehend what I was hearing. He was the one man I'd looked up to my whole life, my hero who'd always taught me right from wrong, and now he was telling me that he'd always known about the dragons. He was a murderer.

He stood so much taller than me, holding his sword by his side. He wasn't standing to fight, but I knew just by looking into his fierce brown eyes that if I drew my own sword, he would raise his. I couldn't beat him. He was the best slayer in the village. But even if I could, would I really have the

281

courage to hold a sword up to my father? Probably not.

We stared at each other, unmoving, for what felt like a lifetime, neither of us backing down and neither of us starting the fight. Uncertainty coursed through me, rendering me unable to make a decision. I was saved by having to do just that by a loud noise and a flash like lightning from outside.

"Dragons!" Jasper came running in. "There are loads of them."

The light I saw must have been one of them shooting fire.

"What have you done? The dragons have never come into the village before. This is all your fault." My father glared at me as if I was a disgrace. If he'd ever looked at me in this manner before, I would have been devastated, but now I didn't care.

I looked him square in the eye. "This is not my fault. The fault rests solely on your shoulders and the other village elders for murdering innocent people. If they have decided to fight back now, then you only have yourselves to blame. Come on, Ash, we have some swords to get."

I ran outside with Ash beside me, leaving my parents behind. The scene we ran into was absolute chaos. Dragons flew overhead, lighting up the night with bursts of fire. The other villagers had heard the noise and were pouring out of their homes to fight. Some were dressed, but most were fighting in their nightwear. There were people everywhere. I saw Ally in his human form engaged in a sword fight with Wolfin, one of my father's best friends. Just behind them, Marcus chased one of the dragons. I could tell by the way it held its wing that it had hurt itself and could no longer fly.

Someone screamed and I saw the faces of two of the village children peering out of a window, watching as their father fought with someone I recognized from Spear's house. Spear himself was nowhere to be seen, but I knew he'd be nearby.

"Some of them have changed into human form," I shouted to Ash as he pulled me through the warring groups, trying to get me to safety.

"They would need to, to get into people's houses to retrieve the swords. I guess this is what they planned once we left."

None of this looked planned. People screamed in pain and bodies littered the ground. Thankfully, no one looked dead. The people I saw on the ground were still moving, but the peaceful raid I'd hoped for was not happening. There was blood everywhere.

Another burst of fire lit up the sky close to where one of the slayers lay prostrate on the ground. I noticed that the dragon missed by a good ten feet. For a second I wondered why, but then realized that he was only using fire for light. Not one of the slayers was burned. It was somewhat a relief, but not using fire in battle would put the dragons at a major disadvantage. It was one of the only weapons they possessed. A dragon in human form swooped in on the back of another dragon. As they passed the man on the ground, the human dragon leaned down and grabbed his sword before flying back into the sky.

I ran to the man. I recognized him as Ben, one of my childhood friends.

"Are you okay?" I asked, kneeling beside him. I couldn't see any blood but his face was contorted in pain.

"I stumbled," he said. "I think I twisted my ankle."

His ankle was already beginning to swell. I turned to Ash. "We need to move him. He's too exposed here."

Ben looked confused as Ash came forward. He obviously didn't realize that Ash was a dragon shifter, but we didn't get many visitors to Dronios. He didn't say anything though, as between us, we managed to get Ben out of harm's way. We dragged him into the first market on the strip.

"You should be OK here," I said, setting him down on a sack of flour. Behind me through the shop window, the sky lit up once again.

"Do you know what's going on?" Ben asked. "There are some humans out there with the dragons. If your friend wasn't with you, I'd have thought he was with them too."

At least it proved that there were more of the villagers that didn't know that the dragons were shifters.

Another scream came from outside.

"Julianna, we need to get out of here."

I turned back to Ben. "No time to explain, but I promise I'll come back when I can and tell everyone everything. Just do me a favor. When this is over, don't listen to my father or the other elders. They've been lying to us for years."

I didn't wait for him to question me further; instead, I took Ash's hand and we ventured back out into the night.

"What now?" I asked. The battle was still going strong, but I wasn't sure what I could do to help. Dragons were battling slayers everywhere I looked, some in their human form with swords and some in their dragon form.

"I think we need to get out of here," replied Ash. "Spear has this under control and us being here is not helping anyone. We're just in the way."

If this was in control, I'd hate to see confusion.

"We can't leave!" I dug my feet into the hard ground, pulling Ash to a stop.

"What do you suggest we do? Fight the dragons or fight the slayers? Because at the moment, I don't see any other option."

He had a point. Fighting on one side would mean hurting the other, and I didn't want anyone hurt. I'd never felt so utterly useless. Running away felt like a betrayal on both sides.

A war cry pierced the air. Out of the darkness, someone came running toward us, sword aloft. Whether it was a dragon coming for me or a slayer coming for Ash, it was too dark to tell. I hesitated. Ash, on the other hand, was ready. He pulled my sword from its sheath and deflected the opposing blade just as it came crashing down, missing me by only an inch. The assailant thrust again, this time going for Ash. I stepped back as the pair fought in the darkness. I could barely see them, although every couple of seconds a burst of light showed me how they were both faring. They were pretty evenly matched. The slayer, and that's what I knew him to be now, was a middle-aged guy from my village, and the best swordsman, but Ash had the advantage of being able to see much better in the dark.

Nerves congregated in my stomach as I watched the fight. I couldn't bear the thought of either of them getting hurt, but I didn't see any other outcome. I didn't know the slayer well, but I knew he was one of the men that regularly went up the mountain. There was no way he would ever back down. I was grateful for the darkness, for without it, Ash would surely be dead by now.

An idea came to me. I ran behind the slayer, praying that no dragon would choose this moment to let out its fiery breath. It would be a disaster if he saw me.

I couldn't see Ash, but I knew he'd be able to see me. I signaled from behind the slayer's back, pointing at his sword and making a motion that Ash should take it. Then I jumped onto the man's back. The shock of someone behind him was enough for him to loosen his grip and for Ash to grab the sword out of his hand. I tried to jump down to run away, but the slayer had already reached over his shoulder and grabbed me by the tunic. I attempted to struggle free, but it was no use. He was much stronger than me. I watched as his other arm came crashing down on me. I cried out as pain shot through my shoulder. I hit him on the head, but it was like a mouse hitting an elephant—I doubt if he even felt it.

A burst of fire illuminated Ash coming towards the man, ready to plunge a sword into him.

"Ash, no!" I shouted. I couldn't let Ash become a murderer for me. I clamped my teeth down hard on the slayer's ear. With a scream, he released me. Ash grabbed my arm and we both ran for our lives toward the path that would lead us out of the village. When the screams and fire were behind us, I let go of Ash's hand so he could change into a dragon.

It was quieter now. I wasn't sure if that was a good or bad sign, but at least the screaming had stopped. Despite all the fire, none of the buildings had burned. Spear had made a mess of this, but he'd kept to his word that they'd try not to hurt anyone. I'd only seen the dragons defending themselves. If they'd used fire for more than the purpose of light, they could have destroyed the village and everyone in it without having to land. It would have been easy to pick through the ashes of the burned down village later for the swords, but doing that would mean the deaths of many, if not all, of the villagers.

They hadn't done that. Of course, it didn't mean no one had been hurt. I'd seen enough to know that there were many injured. I only hoped no one was killed. The dawn was coming and I could see the village better now. Some people were still fighting, but it looked like most of the dragons had left. As I watched, one stretched out its wings and took off into the sky.

"Uh, Julianna," Ash called. I turned to find out why he hadn't changed yet to find his hands in the air and a sword to his throat.

"Jasper!" I cried, seeing who it was that held the sword. "What are you doing?"

"Is it true?"

"Yes. It's true. I've been living among the dragons for the last week. They don't want to hurt anyone."

"They've got a funny way of showing it." Jasper laughed, but it was joyless.

"Look around you. If they wanted to kill anyone, they would have done it. How easy would it be for them to breathe fire and decimate the whole village? They could have done it without even landing, and yet they chose not to. They only want their families back. All those men and women we caught and imprisoned."

Jasper scowled.

"We're the bad guys here," I continued. "We've hunted innocent people for centuries. The dragons have done nothing as we took their people, and yet it is only now that they know that the dragons are only imprisoned and not dead, and now they are doing something about it. Ask yourself why."

"Why should I believe you? You've been with them long enough for them to have brainwashed you. You could be planning to come and murder us all in our beds for all I know."

"You and I have never gotten along very well, and for that I'm sorry. If you don't want to believe me, that's up to you, but I'm asking that you let us go. Papa admitted that he knew about the dragons being shifters right after you left the barn. Maybe you should go talk to him."

I could see he was struggling with what I was telling him, and I couldn't blame him. I could scarcely believe it myself.

"You're lying, you have to be lying." I could see the tears in his eyes and my heart went out to him. I'd just told him that his own father was a murderer. That he was a murderer.

"Papa isn't the only one. I think all the elders know. That's why I'm here—to stop a great injustice that our people have been perpetuating for centuries. Ash's own father was taken by us, and yet not once did he choose to come here and exact revenge. He wants peace as much as I do. You have the choice now. You can be one of them—a coward who lies and murders because of some century-old grievance—or you can do what's right and be on the side of peace."

I held my breath, waiting for him to make his decision, a decision that could mean Ash's death.

Slowly, he lowered his sword to the ground and I exhaled.

"You made the right decision."

His voice wobbled. "I hope for your sake that you're telling the truth because if I find out you are lying to me, I will hunt you both down and plunge this sword into both of your hearts."

"They are telling the truth, Jasper."

I looked around to find my mother standing beside us. She looked exhausted. Her clothes were dirty and ripped and her hair was wild, but she looked unhurt.

"I think you should have this." She handed her sword to me. I tucked it into my belt with mine and the one we had taken from the slayer.

"Thank you."

"It only has one soul in it and it might be no use. You remember the story I told you on your birthday? The dragon was already hurt when I plunged the sword into him. He might have already been dead by the time I did it."

"I appreciate you doing this for us," said Ash. "I want you to know that Julianna did not want any of this."

"I never knew. I wouldn't have let it happen if I had. I want you to know that."

"I know, Mama." I hugged her tightly, tears coursing down both our cheeks.

"Please promise me something," she said as I let her go. "Tell him or her that I'm truly sorry." She nodded at the sword and I knew she was talking about the dragon whose soul was trapped inside.

"I will." I gave her a final kiss on the cheek as Ash turned back into his dragon form. I hopped onto his back and waved as we took off.

As the ground got further and further away, I scanned the village for any dragons. Most had left, but I could see the bodies of three left behind. There was nothing I could do for them now—we had to leave them. I held safe the knowledge that if they had been stabbed by the slayers, at least they wouldn't be dead, only appear that way. Their souls would become imprisoned within the swords, but I knew I was going to come back again and next time, we'd save them all.

CHAPTER TWENTY-FIVE

he early morning sun cast a pink glow on the Triad Mountains making them look spectacular as we flew over them.

A thousand emotions coursed through me as we crested the peak near Frokontas. Guilt about my people, fear of what we would find when we got back to Ash's village. Most of all, I was sad. Sad and utterly exhausted. I yawned as Ash flew lower over the other side of the mountain.

The plan had been to land in the village square, but as we flew over the fire pit by Ash's house, it became apparent that everyone had chosen to land there. Below us was a hive of activity. It looked like the whole town had come out to find out what had happened. Ash circled around a couple of times before landing.

Someone threw him some clothes, so I ran towards Edeline while Ash changed. She was busy bandaging the arm of one of the people who had gone to the village. All around me was chaos—people hurt and bleeding. Someone was shouting, another crying.

"Edeline, what happened?"

"I was going to ask you the same question. Is Ash with you?" Her face held an expression of worry.

"Yeah, he's safe. He's just getting changed. It was a disaster down there. Spear's group managed to wake the whole village. Do you know where he is?"

If anyone knew what had happened, Spear would be it.

Edeline nodded into the crowd. "Last I saw, he was having his foot seen to over there. Just to warn you, he's pretty mad."

He was pretty mad? I was fuming! I found him deep in conversation with another dragon. His right foot was bandaged and I could see he was putting most of his weight on his left.

I butted in, not caring how rude I looked.

"What happened? Wasn't this supposed to be a stealth attack? Do you need me to buy you a dictionary so you understand what stealth means? You couldn't have been noisier if you tried."

"Stop shouting. Come with me." He grabbed me by the arm and took me away from everyone else, to the base of the cliff.

"We did go in silently, but someone saw us. It only took that one person to raise the alarm. You should be happy I kept to my side of the bargain."

"What?" Was he kidding?

299

"None of your people were killed. Just before you rudely butted in, I was talking to Keth. He was the last one to leave the village, just after you. He confirmed that none of your people died. Those that were hurt were only superficially so. They will all live to see another day. Something that can't be said for us. Three of my team were killed." He held up three fingers. "Count 'em. Three! Three dead dragons and you can see the injured." He motioned to the people around the fire pit. It looked like most of those that went down to my village had been hurt in one way or another.

"Oh."

"Oh?" he growled. "Is that all you have to say?"

"Okay, I'm sorry. Thank you. Who...?"

"Ally, Gem and Fiona."

I didn't know Gem or Fiona, but the thought of Ally being hurt was bittersweet. Of course, I didn't want him hurt, but with some luck, the same slayer that pierced him was the one who had captured

Stone. There was a possibility that they were reunited.

"They aren't really dead, though, are they?"

"Oh, well that's okay then," Spear responded with ill-disguised sarcasm.

"You know what I mean. We can get them back. We can get them all back. We just need to find where the bodies are being kept."

"We?" He raised his eyebrow.

"Yes, we! You were right all along. My father knew. He's always known. My whole life has been a lie. Some of the others know too, but not all. I think it's only the village elders. My mother and brother knew nothing about it."

Something else occurred to me then. That's what the eighteenth birthday tradition of killing dragons was all about. It was not just a rite of passage, but also a way to find out who was safe to tell the secret to. Those that killed the dragons willingly joined the hunting group. It was those slayers who would eventually be told about the dragons being shifters. The ones who were bloodthirsty and after years of killing, lacking empathy for the lives of dragons. They were the ones who would be brought into the inner circle. Jasper might not have known the truth yet, but there was no doubt in my mind that he would eventually have found out.

"That's all well and good, but your map was next to useless. After all that, we only managed to recover three swords."

"Four!" I drew my mother's sword from my belt and threw it to him. "This was my mother's. It only holds one dragon, but one dragon is better than none, right?"

"If you think this changes anything, you're wrong. You need to go back to Dronios where you belong."

"No!" I replied forcefully. "You're wrong. I don't belong there. Not anymore. I can do more good here than I can back home. Let me stay. There's so much I can do."

"What can you do?" he spat.

"Pass me my mother's sword back."

"Why?"

"What's happening here?" Ash put his arm around my shoulder.

"Your girlfriend was leaving. Ash, Take her home."

"I wasn't leaving. I was just going to tell Spear that I was going to let him use my blood to release the dragons."

Spear regarded me curiously. "You'd do that?"

"Of course I would. I'm not a slayer anymore." I took a deep breath. "My father was a hero in my mind. Last night I found out he was a murderer. I'm not like him. Most of the villagers in Dronios aren't. Last night, they were defending themselves from an enemy. You have to know that. They need to know the truth and you need me for that. Setting the dragons free will mean nothing if the slayers carry on doing what they're doing. I only have so much blood to release them. Who are you going to use to free them once all my blood is spent?"

"There will be others," Spear stated confidently.

"Other slayers that give up their blood willingly?" I shook my head at the thought.

"Who said it has to be given willingly?" Spear countered.

"What are you saying, Spear?" Ash's arm tightened around me.

"That's not who you are," I said. "The dragons have always been peaceful. This needs to end for good. Peace needs to reign on both sides. We need to educate both sides. It's going to take a lot of work, but we can do it. Together."

"She has a point, Spear," interjected Ash. "This is what I've been saying all along. The people of Dronios are not going to listen to us, but they might listen to her. Without Julianna, we have nothing."

"If she does what she says she will."

The time for words was over. Now was the time for action. I lunged forward and took my mother's sword from Spear. Before he had the chance to stop me, I ran the blade down the palm of my hand. The cut was small, but it was enough. A burst of flame shot out of the end of the sword, sending us all flying backward. The flames swirled into the air, taking on the appearance of a dragon completely made of flames. It spread its wings and flew into the sky. At the very top of the cliff, the flames rearranged themselves and turned into a howling tornado of bright orange fire. Then it disappeared over the top of the cliff.

I picked myself up from the floor where I'd fallen from the intensity of the blast and dusted myself off. One look at Spear's face was enough to tell me that he hadn't expected it to work. His mouth formed a perfect O and he was filthy with dirt from falling to the ground.

Silence rained down on us. I looked over to the others. They might not have seen how it happened, but there was no missing the escaped soul of the dragon. The gaze of the people lowered until a hundred eyes were on me.

"That's right!" I shouted loud enough for them all to hear. "You saw a dragon being freed. I used my own blood." I held aloft my hand to show them the cut I'd made with the sword.

"I've got an apology to make to you all. My father knew all along you were shifters. He's not the only one. There are others. I've never been so angry in my whole life, but this must stop. I'm going to stand with you if you'll let me, and fight this abomination. I'm going to save them all. We are going to save them all. I will not rest until every single dragon is freed."

A couple people began to clap. Then another, then another, until the air was filled with the sound of applause.

"It's not going to be easy," I said when the clapping died down. "What you just saw was the soul of one of your people. That soul is now heading back to the body it came from. That person is going to wake up scared and confused. They're going to be so weak that it will be difficult for them to escape. Fiere flew out from the prison, but I think we can assume that now the elders of Dronios know that we are freeing dragons, they will lock the bodies up more securely and make it impossible to just fly out. The good news is, there are a lot more of us than there are of them, and when the rest of the people in my village know the truth, there will be even more people on our side. Not everyone will believe us and of those that do, some may choose to fight with the elders. It's up to us to convince as many as possible to fight for what is fair and what is right. We need to go back to the village as soon as possible, before they have time to regroup and tell more lies. We need to find where the bodies of the other dragons are kept and free them."

"That could take days," shouted someone.

"Actually, that's going to be the easy part. We have three more swords with dragons trapped inside. You saw yourselves that the souls take the form of fire when outside the body. All we need to do it set one free and be ready to follow it. It will lead us back to the prison. You guys can fly so it should be easy. More than one dragon should go because, after last night, it will be heavily guarded. The biggest problem we face is getting the swords. Look at how many of you were injured and we only got four of them. We need to come up with a better plan."

I looked to where Spear was just pulling himself up from the ground.

"I'm going to be working closely with Spear. Today we will come up with a better plan and this time, I'm going to be more involved." I emphasized the "this time." "Tonight, we go down to the village again and get the swords back. It's going to take more of you than before. I know many of you are not hunters or fighters, but the ten that went there last night wasn't enough. Everyone over eighteen and fit needs to go. We need to swamp them so there is no point in fighting. This has got to end tonight!"

I felt a hand on my shoulder. I turned, expecting to see Ash, but it was Spear. He had a look of grim determination on his face.

"I admit to being wary of Julianna since she first set foot in the village. Why would a slayer help us? But now I see the truth. It takes a great deal of strength and courage to sacrifice yourself for someone else, but it takes a whole lot more courage to stand up to your family. I need those of you who were out last night to rest. The rest of you, be prepared to save our ancestors. We're going in tonight! Who is with us?"

Some of the dragons cheered. Some, like Edeline, looked stunned. But they all raised their hands.

My hand instinctively found the hilt of my sword, like a moth to a flame. The sword that started it all. How quickly my life had changed. Just a few days ago I held this sword with the promise of slaying my first dragon, and today I held it as a promise to save the dragons.

The goblin-made gold held strong as my fingers wrapped around the intricate detail of the handle. With a clean whoosh, I unsheathed my sword and held it out in front of me. The rising sun glinted off the blade as the cheers of the dragons met my ears once again.

Tonight, I would make right all the wrong my ancestors caused. Tonight, I would stand with the dragons and bring their families home.

About J.A. Culican

About J.A. Culican

USA Today bestselling author, J.A. Culican is a teacher by day and a writer by night. She lives in New Jersey with her husband of eleven years and their four young children.

J.A. Culican's inspiration to start writing came from her children and their love for all things magical. Bedtime stories turned to reality after her oldest daughter begged her for the book from which her stories of dragons came from. In turn, the series The Keeper of Dragons was born.

Read More from J.A. Culican

www.jaculican.com

About J.A. Armitage

About J.A. Armitage

Born in a small town, J.A. Armitage longed for adventure and travel.

Age 20 she moved to Dublin, then to San Diego, then Sydney and back to California where she did a brief stint working at Universal Studios being a minder to Sponge Bob.

Once back in Britain she got married, had babies and decided to write about the adventure she was now missing out on. She works full time, is a mum to three kids and has had a surrogate baby.

She has skydived twice (and survived), climbed Kilimanjaro and hiked to the bottom of the Grand Canyon. She has also worked as a professional clown and banana picker amongst other jobs.

Somehow she finds time to write.

Read More from J.A. Armitage

www.jaarmitage.com

Books by J.A. Culican

The Prince Returns - Book 1 in the Keeper of Dragons Series

A mystical calling.

On his 18th birthday, Cole's learns that he is a dragon fated to save all that was deemed true.

Destiny.

Cole's life spirals into an uncontrollable battle for life or death. First, he learns that his family isn't really his own and his birth parents are dragons. With that legacy comes a special calling; devoting an eternity to protecting all true beings from creatures bent on controlling the Earth and bringing an end to dragons.

Danger.

As the newly-minted Prince of Ochana, Cole is also the Keeper of Dragons and his first task is to keep the nefarious farro-fallen fairies-at bay. With no formal training, no control of his mahier-dragon magic, and fear like he's never experienced before, will Cole be able to reach outside of his human side and embrace his destiny in time to defeat the farros?

The Elven Alliance - Book 2 in the Keeper of Dragons Series

The fates have spoken.

Cole and Eva are the Keeper of Dragons - the only ones who can save all true beings from a time of fear.

Uncontrollable power.

Cole finds himself unstable, unpredictable and volatile. He has no control of the tilium-fairy magic he stole from the farros. Out of options, the dragons turn to a once ally - the elves - for help.Curious about the dragon who wields both dragon and fairy magic, they accept -but on their terms only. The dragons must submit to Prince Gaber and his rules.

A new enemy.

Queen Tana continues to haunt Cole's dreams, as a new enemy shows his face - another fallen enemy with a bigger agenda than the farros-fallen fairies; an enemy stronger and smarter; an enemy with an army that could destroy all true beings. Enter King Eldrick of the eldens- the fallen elves.

Sometimes evil wins.

Join international bestselling author, J.A. Culican on an epic fantasy adventure that fans and critics are calling a world of magic, and comparing to Robert Jordan.

Second Sight, Book 1 in the Hollows Ground Series

What if you could foresee death?

Mirela can prophesy the death of whomever she sees. At thirteen, Ela foretold the death of her best friend, only to watch it happen before her very eyes. Ela, now twenty-one, spends her days locked away in her apartment, avoiding the public and the gift she considers a curse.

Until he appears.

Luka Conway is handsome. Charming. And magical. After Ela predicts yet another death, Luka leads her to an underground city hidden beneath Atlanta, populated by empaths, telepaths, and seers. Luka is a Shade, a soldier fighting a secret war against the Wraiths, a deadly group of sorcerers who wish to take over the world. Ela is given no choice; she must prove herself a Shade, and use her powers for the light, or she will be put to death. Resolved to her fate, Ela trains as a warrior, determined to put her curse to good use.

Then Talon Michaels appears. He's just as dashing as Luka, and even more dangerous. A Wraith, Talon warns Ela that the Shades aren't all what they appear. Who can Ela trust, if anyone? Should her powers be used for good...or evil? Which should she choose?

Books by J.A. Armitage

The Labyrinthians

When Kimberley's father loses his job and it looks like her whole family will be homeless, a mysterious old benefactor saves them by leaving his 'mansion' to them in his will. However, their new house, with its history of spooky happenings and disappearances, is not all it seems. When Kim's little brother goes missing, it's up to Kim and her new friend, Nate, to find him. The problem is... When they do - who will find them?

Endless Winter, Book 1 in the Guardians of the Light Series

Imagine falling in love for the first time, the adrenaline, the flutters. Now imagine being told you had to have a baby with somebody else...

Trapped in an unfamiliar room with no way out, Anais has no idea just how much her life is about to change. A locked door stands between her and freedom but as she is just about to find out, the door is the least of her problems.

Anais had never believed in demons and vampires so when she is transported into a dark world that she doesn't understand she is forced to realise that humans can be the most terrifying monsters of all. Yet in the shade of her new life she finds light in the most unexpected place of all.

Made in the USA
Middletown, DE
07 November 2018